I0535566

Love's Memory

A Christian Pioneer Novel

Diana Barclay

All rights reserved. No part of this publication may be reproduced, stored in a retrieval system, or transmitted by any means – electronic, mechanical, photographic (photocopying), recording, or otherwise – without prior permission in writing from the author. This book is a work of fiction. The names, characters, places, and incidents are products of the writer's imagination or have been used fictitiously and are not to be construed as real. Any resemblance to persons, living or dead, actual events, locales or organizations is entirely coincidental.

Copyright © 2015 Diana Barclay

ISBN-13:
978-0692470343 (Lamb Books)

ISBN-10:
0692470344

Dedication

To my sisters, Vicki Peterman and Amy Nyiri.

who inspired me to write for them.

Thank you girls, for not giving up on me and helping me

through this process.

TABLE OF CONTENTS

ACKNOWLEDGMENTS

First, to my husband, Jamie Barclay who supported me throughout this process.

To Abby Pugh, my beautiful niece, who endured a very long photo shoot and became the face of Rebecca.

To Krista Pickard, my amazing niece and personal photographer, who caught my vision and brought it to life.

To Megan Krimmel who made the book even better.

Finally, to my friend, Karen Anna Vogel, who made this dream possible.

.

Chapter 1

Sixteen year old Rebecca O'Donald entered the dark shop in the center of Dublin, Ireland. She quickly opened the shutters to let in light. She briefly stopped to feel the warmth on her face and quickly turned away. She knew better than to linger too long. Rebecca looked around the room and decided it was bright enough for the start of the day. No need to light the lamps. She then busied herself dusting and straightening shelves. It was the same routine each day for as long as she could remember.

As she dusted, a young boy entered the shop and smiled at her. Eric was a nice boy who always tried to talk to her. But she knew if her father saw her show any interest towards the boy she would be sorry later. Besides, even though his eyes seemed kind, weren't all men alike? Just because he was young and showed her kindness now didn't mean that as time passed he wouldn't become an angry, mean man. So, without acknowledging him, she turned back to her work. Receiving no encouragement from Rebecca, the boy chose his purchases and paid Rebecca's father, who gave him a smile. Rebecca knew that smile. It was the one that only came out when there was a customer. Rebecca had often wondered if her father's anger came after a long day because he had to be so polite and obliging to his customers. So, in exasperation, he took it out on his wife and only child.

As Eric left, Rebecca's thoughts wandered, as they often did, into her dream world. She imagined many different scenes of a fantasy that she could only dream about. One such dream was of Eric entering her father's store and boldly claiming her for his wife. He'd be dressed in the richest clothes, and before her father could protest, he would lay a pile of money on the counter. Then, Eric, would walk over to her and bow. He would tell her that he loved her and ask her to be his wife. In her dream, she would not hesitate even a moment, but drop the duster and take her love's hand and walk out of the shop into the sunlight and a new life.

Without realizing it she bumped into a jar of fruit and it went flying to the floor. She cried out at the sounds of the shattering glass, as she realized the consequences of her daydreaming. Oh, how clumsy she was! Would she ever learn to do the right thing? She looked up at her father to see his face darken with fury. She leaned down to pick up the glass with nervous hands when she sensed her father standing above her.

"Oh, Papa, I'm so sorry," she said hoping to ward off what would come next, but knowing that nothing would change his mind.

"That cost me money you clumsy oaf!" he growled. Rebecca dared not look up as she closed her eyes as the booted foot came and met her stomach. She cried with pain and gasped as she lost her breath. As he dragged her to her feet she cried out from the pain of his grasp on her arm. Rebecca looked up at him as the rage showed in his dark blue eyes.

"You be careful with the merchandise, ya' hear!" he yelled.

"Yes, Father," she whimpered. He formed his large hand into a fist and knocked her in the face causing her to move away from him with a great force. She cried and reached up to her cheek as he pulled her back toward him.

"Now clean up this mess and there won't be any supper for you to make up for the loss," he grumbled in her ear. He released her with a push and she careened with the shelf. He turned back to the counter and as the bell tinkled at the door to signify a customer he straightened his smock and brushed back his thinning gray hair and said with a smile, "Good afternoon, Mrs. Darcy. How are you this fine day?"

Tears of pain and anger poured from Rebecca's eyes and dripped to the floor mingling with the juice from the fruit. She gingerly picked up the glass, hardly able to see from the tears.

She got a scrub brush and soapy water and scrubbed the floor. She tried to conceal her pain from the customer, knowing that one word from Mrs. Darcy could mean more wrath after she left.

After Mrs. Darcy had made her purchases and left father and daughter alone in the store again, her father came over to inspect the area that Rebecca had cleaned and humphed. Rebecca quivered in the corner as far from him as she dared and gave a sigh of relief at the sign that it was acceptable and returned to her dusting but not to the daydreaming. The pain in her stomach and face kept her from thinking of anything else but keeping her concentration on her work.

~*~

Rebecca's stomach growled. The shop was closed and her parents had gone to the back part of the store where the family lived. She continued to do the work her father had given her before he left to eat his supper. She looked around her, the room was full of food and yet she stood there hungry. Hot tears came to her eyes as she weakly dragged boxes from the stock room and restocked shelves. She was so thin from the little food that was given to her that missing one meal left her weak and dizzy. She knew if she did not eat that there was a good chance she would pass out. If it was left up to her father he'd let her starve to death, she realized. A strong desire for survival welled up inside of her and she began looking around for something to eat. If she didn't take care of herself, no one would.

She could not help noticing the apple that had been neglected in the bin. It was turning brown and would be rejected by the customers. Surely she could eat it. Would her father notice it was gone? Her stomach seemed to gnaw at her insides and hunger overcame fear as she reached for the apple and put it to her lips smelling the sweetness of it. Oh, how she loved fruit! But she rarely received any and only when it had been rejected by others. She bit into it and a smile came to her face as the juice ran down her chin. She ate quickly, with one eye on the doorway to the living area. She ate all but the few parts that were inedible and quickly hid the remains in the pocket of her frock. The apple did calm some of the gnawing in her stomach and she returned to her work. She worked on into the night and began to wonder if her father had forgotten her. Would he leave her there all night? She fought off the drowsiness until she finally succumbed and placed her head on her arms on the counter. Just for a moment, she said to herself, but before she knew it she had been asleep for quite a while.

She was awakened by a bellow, "You lazy girl!" She jerked into a standing position. Her father, spewing obscenities, slapped her so hard that she flew across the room and crashed into a display of sewing items that poured onto the floor. He grabbed her arm and pulled her up, "Now look what you did!" he scowled. She could smell the whiskey on his breath and knew that she would not escape his worst wrath that night.

She quickly ran to the display to start picking up the spilled pins and needles. Her father walked toward her with his hands clenched. She begged him to stop. "I'm sorry, Father, I'm sorry!" she cried, almost in hysteria, now.

He began hitting his only child again and again. Words spewed from his mouth cutting to Rebecca's very soul. "You are worthless. I never wanted a child but that ungrateful wife of mine had you. Now I have to put up with you and your clumsiness. Well, I won't anymore. As soon as I find someone to take you off my hands, I'll say good riddance to you." As he hit her again and again, she tried to cover her face with her hands, but it was useless. Rebecca finally did escape the verbal and physical abuse as a swirl of blackness covered her.

Hours later, Rebecca roused to find herself lying on the floor in the midst of the sewing items that had spilled earlier. She winced and cried out in pain, crawling to the counter and pulled herself up to her feet. She limped into the living area, and slowly made the ascent up the steps to her room. Crawling into her bed and pulling her legs up tight to her chest, she cried herself to sleep.

Her mother came to awaken her a few hours later. There was a tear in her eye as she looked at her beloved child's bruised and cut face.

Rebecca tried to open her eyes but every part of her being cried out to stay in the dark place that she was in. Her mother's cries and encouragement made her open them. She had trouble opening her right eye for it was swelled. She looked through bleary eyes at her mother who also nursed bruises.

She saw her mother cry and reached up to hug her. "I'm so sorry, my child, I wish that I could find a way for you to escape all this," the older woman whispered. "He's worse when he's drunk, y'know, and after supper last night a customer came to the door and invited him out for the evening. He threatened to beat me if I didn't leave you in the shop until he returned."

Rebecca did not answer or acknowledge her mother's words but clung to her like a small child who had been lost and then found. Rebecca and her mother knew that something had to be done. The beatings were getting worse and Rebecca was getting thinner from the repeated forced fasting. But neither daughter nor mother knew what to do.

The pair quickly went down to the kitchen, grateful at least that the man they both feared would not be rising for a few hours as he slept off the whiskey.

That day, with Clarence passed out in his bedroom, Rebecca and her mother were left in the shop together. It was at least a little comforting to know after a drinking spell and a beating, Rebecca would have some peace the following day.

She had trouble walking from the beating and limped around the room. The doorbell tinkled and she looked up to see a woman that had tried to talk to her mother about God. Her mother had always been too timid to talk to her with her husband in the shop. But today she knew she would not see him for several hours. So she asked Rebecca to run the store and invited the woman back to the kitchen for tea.

Rebecca stood in the doorway and listened to the conversation whenever there was no one to wait on. She heard the cries of her mother and the woman trying to console her. Rebecca leaned closer to the doorway and eaves-dropped.

"I'm just so afraid that one of these days he will kill her."

"Can't you leave him?" the stranger asked.

"How can I? He knows everyone in town. He will hunt us down and kill me for sure. Something has to be done."

"Margaret, do you believe in prayer?"

"Yes, as a child I went to church regularly. But lately I have not had the faith to believe in anything."

"Let's pray that God will intervene in your daughter's life and make a way of escape for her."

"All right, I can pray for that."

8

A customer entered the shop, so Rebecca did not hear the rest of the conversation. But she wondered about those parts she had heard. She knew that her mother had often prayed for release from her suffering, but God had not answered. Would He answer now? Would she be rescued before it was too late she wondered. She did not know much about God. Why would He do anything for her? She was a clumsy girl and deserved the punishment she received from her father.

The woman only stayed a few minutes longer before she walked back into the shop and bid Rebecca and Margaret good-bye.

"It will be okay," she promised as she left.

Margaret looked at her daughter who had the same auburn hair as her own, "It will be okay. We prayed for God to make a way of escape for you."

Rebecca's father returned to working in the shop the next day. He made no comment of the events of the previous days, nor said much to Rebecca. The family got back into a routine as the women nursed their wounds back to health.

~*~

A week later, a man Rebecca had seen her father talk to in whispered tones several times that week entered the shop again. He was a short man, who looked as round as he was tall. Though yet early in the morning, he took out a handkerchief to wipe sweat from his face. He appeared to be the same age as her father with graying temples, a big nose, and beady eyes. He seemed nervous and again spoke in whispers to her father. Although the beady-eyed man kept looking at her, Rebecca ignored the pair and continued in her work concentrating on what she was doing. She did not dare have a repeat of her prior mistake of daydreaming.

Eventually, the man left with an "I'll be back this evening," being the only words spoken loud enough that Rebecca could hear.

That evening, Rebecca helped her mother clean up after a quiet meal, the best kind of meal where her father kept his wrath to himself and Rebecca could eat in peace. It was a rare moment for the family and Rebecca wondered what had kept her father so silent. She finished every bite of the meager amount of food that was given to her. She seemed never to have enough and her thin body revealed the lack of a healthy diet.

There was a knock on the back door and Mr. O'Donald rose and invited in the round little man from that morning. He led him into the small kitchen as the man kept his eyes on Rebecca. Her stomach rolled as she looked at him and then she quickly averted her eyes from the man. Mr. O'Donald offered him a seat, but he continued to stand not taking his eyes off of Rebecca. She became uneasy and tried not to fidget.

"Pretty hair, isn't it?" her father stated nodding his head toward Rebecca.

"Can't see much of it!" the stranger growled.

"Girl, take down your hair," her father commanded.

Rebecca gasped and fumbled with the pins. But she had grown very nervous and could not manage. Her mother quickly joined her and had the pins out quickly as the long curly hair cascaded down over Rebecca's shoulders. The man went over and touched her hair with a wicked smile, "Pretty hair, indeed!" Rebecca shuddered and fought the urge to run from the room. Instead she closed her eyes.

The man scoffed at her reaction and dropped his hand.

"Might skinny, isn't she?" the man demanded.

"Skinny, but strong. She be able to lift stock in the shop."

"She's too small to have babies!"

Mr. O'Donald grabbed his wife by the arm and pulled her to his side, "My wife is small, and she had no trouble birthin' the girl. She's young and will grow some, too."

The man nodded his head as if in acceptance to the reasoning. "I don't want no bossy woman telling me what to do!"

"There are ways to keeping her lips shut if you know what I mean!" Her father said with a wicked grin, as he winked at the man. "But no need to worry about this one; I have her well trained."

"Alright, I'll take her," the man said, as if she was a piece of merchandise in the store, "I want her tonight!"

This time Rebecca's mother gasped and immediately was sorry as her husband gave her a scowl and tightened the hold on her arm.

Mr. O'Donald nodded at the man, "I knew you would so I've arranged for a minister to come over tonight. He'll be here soon."

"Woman," he said turning to his startled wife, "help her get her things."

The women quickly obeyed and went to the small room that had been Rebecca's only refuge. Her parent's room was downstairs, and her father rarely took the effort to climb up the steps. The room had only a bed covered with a worn blanket, one crate for Rebecca's meager belongings and one she used for a chair.

After shutting the door, Rebecca's mother whispered, "I did not know." Seeing tears in her daughter's eyes, "It could not be any worse than here. Maybe this is your way of escape."

Rebecca shuddered at the thought that this horrible little man could be the answer to her mother's prayer. But knowing there was no use in discussing it or arguing about it, the two silently placed Rebecca's meager possessions in an old crate. Each wished to express their thoughts and heart to the other, but neither were able to do so. Turning to leave, Mrs.

O'Donald embraced the only joy in her life and wept for a few moments until she heard her husband bellowing for them to hurry up. Rebecca clung to the thin, tired woman for only a moment longer, knowing that any delay would cause trouble for her mother later. Rebecca could see volumes of unspoken words in her mother's dull blue eyes and they turned to leave the room. Rebecca did not turn back for even one last peek. She knew from years of abuse that remorse was to no avail, and she had learned to take each moment of her life in stride. What could be worse waiting for her outside this home than what she had already endured at her father's hand? Could she finally be released from the suffering that she had experienced ever since she could remember?

Maybe her mother's prayers had been answered. But what of her mother's own suffering? Rebecca could only hope with her not there to antagonize her father, he might be easier on his wife. After all it had been her own clumsiness that had caused the beatings, and with her gone, her father would not have any reason to get so angry.

The minister was waiting with the two men and looked surprised at the youngness of Rebecca's face, but he did not voice his reservation. Rebecca stood beside the man called Richard McNeal. She cast her eyes down at the floor and listened as the minister spoke, and she answered yes at the appropriate time. It was soon over, and the minister was paid and quickly retreated leaving the remaining four standing there. Rebecca noticed that the minister was not the only one being paid that day, for she saw Richard reach into his money bag again and give her father a fistful of money. She thought with remorse of her dream of a better future. Without a word, Richard took Rebecca by the arm and led her out of the house. She looked back only briefly for her last look at her mother, and a tear fell down her face.

Richard rushed her to the street and into a waiting carriage. He looked at her with a lustful grin and placed his hand on her leg. She grimaced but forced herself not to move away. She smiled at him. Though scared, she knew that the next few hours could make or break her relationship with this man who had just become her husband. She was determined not to do anything that would incur his wrath.

But her determination to be accommodating to him was to no avail. The carriage driver called to his horses to stop. They were in front of a hotel near the water front. Richard got out. She followed him with her few belongings in her arms. He ushered her past the desk and up the stairs. He walked quickly for such a short man, and she had trouble keeping up with him. She stumbled once, and he just growled at her. At the top of the steps he stopped for a moment to catch his breath and wipe the sweat from his face. He looked at her, and she took a step back away from him. He laughed and walked to a door and removing a key from his pocket, unlocked the door and walked in.

Rebecca stood frozen where he had left her. He turned and scowled at her, and she found the courage to follow him into the room, her heart pounding with fear.

The room was clean but sparse. It had a bed and a table with a pitcher and basin setting on it. Rebecca eyed the bed fearfully and instinctively backed away. With one swift move Richard closed the door of the room and grabbed Rebecca. "Come here you little wench," he exclaimed as he slapped her. "Your father seems to think this is how I keep you in line." She cried out as she was flung to the floor.

"I'll do as you say," she whimpered. But Richard gave her no chance to obey; he grabbed her and dragged her to the bed. He clawed at her dress, and her hope of a peaceful marriage was shattered. Earlier, she had foolishly thought what could be worse than life at her father's hands. But now she realized there were worse things in a woman's life than beatings.

As he slept, later, beside her with one arm on top of her as if he was afraid of her running off, she wept silently into her pillow and resigned herself to a life no better than the one she had come from and most likely even worse.

Through the night, he repeated the earlier abuse, becoming more violent with each time, until he finally lay silently, and she closed her eyes in exhaustion and grief and dozed.

The next morning, she woke up exhausted and trembling. She dared not move for fear of waking him up and getting more of his "husbandly attention". Her mind cried out for help. The woman who visited her mother had said to pray to God for an answer. Rebecca had refused to pray then, but now, she felt even more hopeless and alone. Dared she pray to this God she did not know? Would He answer the prayers of a wicked girl like her? She had caused her father to do so many evil things. What was it about her that made men react so violently to her? Would God listen to her? Somehow she knew she had no other way of escape and so she cried out to God to show her what to do. But no answer came.

Chapter 2

*W*hen hours went by and her new husband did not rouse. She looked at him and wondered why he looked so strange. His skin had a gray pallor about it and he was completely still. Her heart began to beat quicker as fear leapt inside of her.

"My goodness! He looks dead!" she thought. She dared to reach out a solitary finger and touch the skin on his arm, half fearful that she would awaken him and he would continue where he'd left off, and half afraid he wouldn't move at all. Putting forth all of the courage she could muster, she reached out and touched him and then withdrew her hand in a flash. It was just as she'd expected...he was cold!

The shock overcame her as she realized he was dead. "I have killed him," she cried and began to weep uncontrollably. She was most definitely a wicked girl if her own husband would die in her bed. The stress and fatigue of the past hours overwhelmed her, and a fear rose up inside of her. She knew that she would be blamed for his death and unsure of what that meant, she cried in hopelessness.

Eventually, she came to her senses and realized that she had to leave the room before anyone came looking for the man. She knew one thing: she was not returning to her father's home. She gingerly searched the man's pockets for the money bag she had seen the evening before. She found it and took out a wad of bills and two tickets for what appeared to be a passage on a ship to America. She saw the date and realized that the tickets were for that very day!

Who was this man called Richard McNeal? What type of man carried a wad of cash around in his pocket? Was he running away from something or someone? He was obviously in a hurry to have married Rebecca practically "sight unseen." Who or what would be waiting in that far away, foreign country? Family, friends, a job? Or perhaps a vast land of empty faces where a person could get lost in and never be found...if he or she were being sought.

Was she in danger by staying at his side? "Come on, Rebecca, calm down!" she said to herself. She had to form a plan. She had nothing to stay for and the tickets seemed to be the answer. She'd go to America in hope of a better life! Yes, that's what she'd do!

"The tickets are mine, now," she rationalized. Hadn't she paid the price many times over throughout the night of terror? Was she not in fact Mrs. Richard McNeal?" The very name made her shudder and gave her an even stronger determination to escape.

Her plan began to take shape as she left some money in the man's pocket, hoping when found it would not appear that she had robbed him. But really, she was his wife, she thought as if still trying to convince herself. Didn't she have a right to his money and the tickets?

She looked at herself in the mirror. She gingerly touched the swollen bruise on her face and gasped at the girl looking back at her. It was the same face as her mother's, pale, tired, and oh so old.

She realized that she could not travel in the ragged clothes she had on, not with these tickets she supposed were for first class.

But wouldn't someone suspect a young girl traveling without a chaperone? A plan was quickly formed. She found a general store and made a few purchases. She tried to be discreet but no one gave her a notice anyway. The shop was crowded with hurried travelers. She returned to the little room and did not even glance at the man on the bed who she had covered with the quilts. She looked at her form in the mirror and pulled her hair up tightly on top of her head. She donned trousers, a white shirt, a cap and boy's shoes. She stared at her transformation in the mirror. Would she be able to pull off this facade? She stared at the boy in the mirror who looked familiar with her own dark blue eyes. She giggled at the thought of pretending to be a boy and with a slightly masculine voice, she practiced speaking to strangers. When she felt that she was presentable, she stuffed her dresses down deep in the man's valise and placed another new shirt and trousers on top.

Without a backward glance at her husband, she peeked out the door, seeing no one in the hall, she snuck out and down the steps, out the door, and down the street until she felt that she was a safe distance from the hotel.

She walked toward the wharf. She showed her ticket to people along the way and they pointed her to the right ship. Her heart pounded with the knowledge of what she was doing. She had never been on her own before. She had never truly made a decision in her entire life. She had obeyed her father's every command. Was her heart pounding with excitement or fear? She admitted it was from both. She was excited about the freedom that lay ahead of her but frightened over the prospect of making decisions that could affect her life. She was going to a strange land with no plans and no one to meet her. What was she doing? She considered turning back and going home. She wasn't ready to be on her own. She was only sixteen and had never been farther than her own street.

A scene flashed before her as she remembered the last beating she had endured, and she knew she could not return. She picked up her step as she dodged other travelers along the way. She glanced at the faces of the other travelers. Where were they going? Were they escaping a nightmare like she was?

The dock was crowded with people ready to board. With the congestion and confusion, she had no trouble boarding. She hardly noticed how massive the ship was before her as she approached the gang plank.

"Ticket, please," the man barked.

Rebecca held out one of the tickets, willing her hand not to shake. She almost gasped as she looked at her obviously feminine hands. She had decided if any one did ask about her, she would tell them she was traveling with her father and that he boarded at a different time. The man only looked at the ticket briefly before he looked behind her to bark orders to seamen loading a huge crate. He handed her the ticket, and without another glance at her, told her where her cabin was and then continued to give the men instructions.

Rebecca pushed past him and stumbled up the gang plank to the ship. She looked around and tried to get her bearings. For a few moments she stood at the railing and watched people saying good-bye to their loved ones. She tried to swallow the knot in her throat at the thought of leaving her mother and never seeing her again. She wished that there was some way to tell her mother that she had escaped.

With that wish came the realization that the prayer had been answered! She had escaped her father just as her mother and the kind woman had prayed! Oh, how she wished God had rescued her mother as well. She could only hope that her leaving would bring a reprieve to her mother's suffering.

She envied the little families saying their farewells and their apparent closeness. Could she ever have someone to love her like that? Tears welled up behind her eyes. How could she expect to ever find love? She was too wicked, too ugly. No. All she could hope for is to find a place to live in America and be free from her father's beatings and her dead husband's abuse. Rebecca angrily wiped the tears from her eyes and turned away from the happy scenes around her. No use longing for what she could not have. She should be grateful to God for being rescued at all.

She made her way to the small cabin her husband had paid for as she felt fatigue wash over her, not realizing how tired she was. Her nerves were on end, and she could bear no more. She was pleasantly surprised to find the room neat and clean with two berths and even a porthole.

Most of all, she reveled in being alone with no threat from her father or her husband. She felt a wave of sadness thinking about her mother. She knew that she would never see her again. She lay down on the bunk and with the gentle rocking of the ship fell into a much needed sleep.

Chapter 3

Austin Finnigan held his first born son in his arms and looked at him with pride. He counted his fingers and toes: all accounted for. He rubbed the matted hair of the newly born child. For a moment he reveled in this new life given to him. Then, he handed the child to the plump older woman standing behind him. She carried the child from the room and closed the door behind her.

Austin's revelry was soon replaced with deep depression as he looked down at his wife now lying peacefully. There was no sign on her face of the struggle that she had just been released from, nor of the battle for which she fought and lost her life.

Austin fell to his knees and wept at his beloved wife's side. He did not know how he could go on without her since he'd loved her so deeply from the very first moment when he had laid eyes on her at a small church back in Ireland. He had wooed her and convinced her to go with him to America. They had struggled to survive there until Austin found a job with other men, building the railroad westward across the Great Plains. He had made good money and soon had saved up enough to get a parcel of land with some left over to buy lumber and build his wife a decent home. At the thought of the three-roomed home he had built for her, he wept bitterly at his loss.

Eventually, his thoughts returned to the present, and he looked at his wife. How peaceful she looked, he mused. He knew that she was at peace now in heaven with her Lord to whom she had devoted her life. But how could she leave him with four children to raise?

Austin touched her red hair and sun-tanned skin. Oh how she loved to work outdoors in the garden. Well, now she was in a place that was full of light and peace. With a resolve, Austin stood, combing his hands through his brown hair as he did when he was thinking or felt nervous. His green eyes took one last look at his beloved bride, then covered her face with a sheet and opened the door only to be barraged by questions from his children.

Seven year old twins, Carrie and Kristie wrapped their arms around him as he closed the door behind him. He stood in the main room that had a rocker, a fireplace, and other wooden chairs. From that room he looked into the kitchen area to see Mrs. White tending the baby. He picked up both girls in one swift motion and carried them to the rocker. He sat down, gave them a hug, and made room for five year old Kelly Anne to sit down with him. All three girls had the same red hair as their mother but sported Austin's green eyes and long face.

The woman at the sink, now dressing the baby, breathed a prayer of wisdom for the newly widowed father.

"Girls," he began, "what do you think of your new little brother?"

"He's all wrinkly," said little Kelly.

Austin smiled at her and held her closer.

"Can I hold him?" asked Carrie.

"I want to first," demanded Kristie. "I'm the oldest." Kristie was always reminding Carrie that she was five minutes older.

"Everyone will have a chance," Austin said wearily, "But first we must talk about Mama." He hesitated, grasping for some way to broach the hardest conversation he'd ever have with his children.

"Do you remember what heaven is?"

"That's where people go when they die. Jesus is there waiting for them to hug them. That's what Mama says!" Carrie announced proudly.

"You're right, honey, and now that's where your mama is."

25

"But people don't come back from heaven, Papa. Do they?" cried Kristie.

"No, honey, they don't. Mama is in heaven with Jesus. She will not be coming back."

The twins tried to comprehend what their father had said, stared at him for a while, and then Carrie burst into tears. The other two girls did the same. Austin allowed them to cry as he too joined them in their grief.

Austin led the children off to bed, tucked them in, and listened to their prayers. He almost started weeping again when Carrie prayed that Jesus would take good care of their mama. He sat with the girls for a while until he heard their steady breathing in sleep and then returned to the living room. Mrs. White was now sitting in the rocker with the baby.

Austin looked at her, searching her eyes for some solace, some answer. He saw compassion there but no answer. He strode over to her and looked at the child in her arms.

"Do you want me to take him home with me?" she said softly. She was older than Austin with graying hair and quick brown eyes that seemed to always know what was going on and what someone needed.

Austin reached out and touched the tiny head. "No, we'll manage. I'm not new at this. I helped Victoria when the twins came. I'm sure I can manage," he said with more confidence then he felt. "It's my fields I'm worried about, but I can take the children with me. They like to play in the grass and look for critters. Besides, it should only be a few days. I'm expecting my little sister to arrive from Ireland any day now. She had promised to come help Victoria with the new baby."

Mrs. White smiled, "Okay, then, it's settled. I'll help you as best I can. Don't worry about bread and the such; I'll be bringing ya some on a regular basis until she comes and gets settled."

"I'd appreciate the extra help. I'm not much for baking and cooking."

"How will you feed the baby?"

"When the twins were born, Victoria did not have enough of her own milk, so she got bottles for them. We still have those bottles left."

"Okay, then," Rose seemed reluctant to go.

Austin put his hands out for the baby, "We'll be okay. I suppose we'll have to…" he hesitated caught up with emotion, "umm… arrange Victoria's burial tomorrow. Will you send one of the boys to tell the others?"

"Of course. I'll see you first thing in the morning to help with preparing the body." She handed the baby to Austin and he held him close. "Good night, Austin. My prayers are with you."

Austin walked her to the door without another word. After she had left, he carried the baby to the rocker. He should have put him down in his cradle, but he did not want to be alone. He rocked the baby and sang lullabies to him trying to forget about the body in the next room but never succeeding.

Austin was still in the rocker the next morning when Mrs. White returned. He looked at his tired, blood shot eyes and knew that he had a rough night. She reached for the baby, and Austin gave him up reluctantly. Mrs. White placed the baby in the cradle and turned to prepare the body. Austin continued to sit in the rocker staring at the fire. The girls stirred and came out to the living area. Austin did not acknowledge them.

"Papa, we're hungry," complained Kelly Anne as she tried to crawl into his lap. Austin snapped out of it and smiled at the little girl. He wanted so much to die from the pain that was in his heart. But he had far greater responsibilities standing before him. He rose and carried Kelly Anne into the kitchen and prepared the children oatmeal.

The funeral was a blur to Austin. He did what was expected of him but it was all mechanical. He felt distant from his body as if watching another man go through the steps. His beloved was gone, but he could not comprehend it. He half expected to see her come over the grassy hill giggling with flowers in her hands.

He thanked those who attended, and then he was gratefully alone. But not alone. He must see to the children. They were quiet. The baby was quiet. The girls stood huddled together gazing at their father. He didn't look at them, he did not tickle them, he did not laugh, and because of his manner, fear filled their hearts. He was so blinded by his own grief that he did not see theirs.

But as children are persistent, soon he found all three on his lap clinging to him. There they sat before the fire rocking, staring, silent.

The next morning Austin fed the children, placed the baby in a basket and headed for the fields. He kept his thoughts from dwelling on the fresh mound of dirt on the little knoll above the field. He refused to think of anything but the task of the moment. Days went by with the same routine.

In the midst of routine, Austin found little comfort for his pain. He kept to himself and didn't even go to church. He refused above all to pray or read the Bible. Both of those activities had been a consolation to him in the past. He had relied on the Lord when he left his beloved Ireland and sailed to America with a new wife. He had relied on the Lord when there was a drought and crops dried up. He had relied on the Lord when the news came by wire that his father had passed on, and he was unable to join his mother and sister and console them. Now, though, his hurt was too deep. At least that was what he tried to convince himself. He did not want to be consoled. Austin did not want to go on. He did not want to feel God's peace. He wanted to grieve. When he would allow himself to consider what was going on with him, he realized that above all the true problem was his anger at God. Hadn't he served Him? Hadn't he prayed for help? Where was God when he needed Him? He refused to consider what he already knew, and though the verses came to his mind of how through trial God was with him, that through the fire we will not be burned, or the thought that Victoria was in a far greater place, he would push them aside with anger and dig deeper into his work.

The children sensed their father's anger and seemed to cling to him in fear and misunderstanding, but he was too wrapped up in himself to notice.

Chapter 4

Hours after boarding the vessel, Rebecca stirred as she dreamed. She was working in the shop and heard someone enter. A man with compassionate eyes stood before her. She turned to look at him, and he smiled at her. Her father went to greet the man. The man ignored her father and did not take his eyes from Rebecca. She felt all the hurt and pain from abuse flow from her body as she gazed into those eyes. He reached out his hand, and she took it. He said, "I have come to rescue you. You are mine now. You do not belong here. You never did. I have come to take you back."

It was a daydream that Rebecca had used to escape the reality of life with her father. This time, it seemed to be more than just a daydream. She woke up and felt deep in her heart that it was a promise, a promise of peace. Somehow she knew that it was from God; the same one who had rescued her was promising a better life for her. Tears formed in her eyes at the thought of finally escaping the pain of her short life.

She climbed down off the bunk with a bounce in her step. She retrieved some food that she had bought at the shop where she had purchased the clothes. Rebecca ate and ate until full and smiled at the strange sensation. But just as quickly, nausea set in, and she lost the whole meal to the chamber pot.

Feeling hot and needing some fresh air, she went up on board and stood at the railing for quite a while. She took a few deep breaths and began to feel better. She looked out and saw only ocean. There was no more sign of her home country, even in the distance. Would she miss Ireland? She had known little of it but the shop and the home in which she was born. Her heart cried out for the one who had raised her, brushed her hair, secretly made time to play a game with her, and taught her how to cook and take care of the home. Yes, she would miss Ireland and her mother most of all, but she was hopeful for a better life in America.

Rebecca turned her face away from the past and looked toward the future. She stood a while, watching the waves and listening to their steady crashing on the ship. She still felt the peace she had experienced in the dream and closed her eyes to picture the face of the man. The face of God? She could only remember his eyes and on those she concentrated. When she opened her eyes she noticed a young girl standing beside her staring at her. She blinked and turned to go, not wanting to give herself away by talking to anyone.

The girl gave her no chance to escape, but walked up to her boldly, and whispered, "You're not a boy, you're a girl."

Rebecca gasped and stared at the girl, not sure what to do or say. The girl was of the same height as Rebecca, but seemed to hold herself up with confidence that gave her an appearance of being older than she actually was. The wind whipped at her brown hair, but she ignored the strands of hair flapping in her face. Finally, Rebecca regained her composure and turned away. Her head was swimming with what to do next. She began walking toward her cabin.

She sighed with relief when the girl did not follow her. When she got to her cabin door, they were serving food in the community room. She took her portion of food and water and went into her cabin. This time she sipped the water slowly and took smaller bites. Her mind flashed back to the day she nibbled on a piece of old fruit and smiled. She could eat what she wanted now.

She wondered about the girl she met on deck. How was she going to keep avoiding her? She had quite a long journey ahead of her. It was inevitable that she would see the girl again. She decided she wouldn't hide the truth. At least not the fact that she was a girl and not a boy.

~*~

Sure enough, it didn't take long until Rebecca saw the girl again the next evening. "Your secret is safe with me! My name is Erin. What's yours?"

"Rebecca," she croaked.

"Why are you pretending to be a boy?" the quizzical girl asked.

Rebecca looked all around her and then back to the gentle green eyes of the girl, "I was afraid of being a girl traveling alone."

"Oh...why are you traveling alone?"

Rebecca could not believe the girl's forwardness and chose to ignore the question.

Erin didn't seem to notice that Rebecca had not given her a response and went on, "I'm traveling alone, too. I'm going to America. My brother sent for me. His wife has been sickly, and he thought I could help her with the children. She has three already with one set of twins. She's expectin' soon. I hope I get there in time for the birthing. I'd love to see a new born baby. Have you seen a baby being born?" Without waiting for a response she continued to ramble on, "I never did. I'm the youngest in the family. Sure now, Mama was hard pressed to let me go, but Austin said it would be a good start for me to be in America. He has a big farm in the West. He says there are lots of young men looking for young ladies to marry. I might not even be there for very long before I'm a mama myself."

She looked at Rebecca, whose eyes were large with surprise at the girl's incessant talking.

"I'm sorry, have I been talking too much? Mama tells me all the time that I talk too much. I try, but I always seem to have something to say and since you weren't doing much talking, I thought I'd just talk. Where are you staying? I'm staying below deck. All of those women and crying babies! It's already so stuffy down there I can hardly breathe."

Rebecca's head was spinning. She did not know if it was from the ship, the events of the past twenty four hours, or the fast talking of the brunette in front of her. With all of her overbearing personality, Rebecca liked Erin immediately, so she said guardedly, "I have one of the staterooms."

Erin looked at her and her outfit and asked, "I feel safe traveling as a woman. They separate the men below from the families and single women. Why don't you put a dress on?"

~*~

Rebecca was already feeling uncomfortable in the trousers and wished that she could change back into one of her comfortable dresses, but they were ragged and patched. She could not pass as someone that could afford a cabin on a ship.

"I have nothing to wear that is fitting," she said ashamed.

"That's not a problem, for sure, I brought more that I could ever use. Why don't we go down and see what you like?"

With that, Erin turned and headed toward the women's hatchway. Rebecca followed meekly. As they descended, Rebecca's eyes took a moment to focus in the dark steerage section. There were bunks stacked on top of each other with just a mattress on each. Some women had brought bedding with them. Others only had bare stained mattresses. The smell, even though early in the voyage, took her breath away, and she gasped.

Erin quickly went to her trunk that was in the aisle beside her bunk and opened it. It was full of dresses. Rebecca had never thought anyone could have that many.

Erin dug down until she found one she thought would be a good one for Rebecca. Erin held it up to her, nodded her head, and handed it to her.

"There, that should work for now!" she smiled.

Rebecca smiled weakly, "I've never had anything as beautiful as this."

"Let's go to your room so that you can try it on," replied Erin.

They made their way to the staterooms and into the room that now seemed spacious. Rebecca looked around at the two bunks with a mattress and linens. There was a washbasin and even drawers. She thought about where Erin was staying and said, "Do you want to come and stay with me?"

"Could I?" Erin exclaimed, "That would be wonderful. I had to share my bunk with two other women! We could be roommates. We could stay up and talk all night."

Rebecca was already beginning to regret her offer, but when the girl smiled at her, Rebecca felt an uncanny drawing toward her. The girls decided that they needed to be careful bringing Erin's things to the room, and that they would go in the morning when the women were out on deck.

~*~

In the meantime, Rebecca turned her attention to the blue dress with white dainty flowers that Erin had given her. Rebecca touched the frock lovingly tracing the lace around the square neck and on the edges of its puffy sleeves. "Thank you for the dress, Erin. It's beautiful."

Rebecca went to her satchel and gathered more appropriate undergarments and changed out of the boy clothing, being careful how she dressed so that Erin would not see the bruises. Then she laid the dress on top of the drawers for the next day and stuffed the boys clothing into the satchel.

Then she clamored up into her bunk and laid her head down on the pillow. Erin followed suit onto the other bunk and much to Rebecca's surprise, was sleeping in a few minutes. She was grateful that Erin did not follow through on her promise to talk all night and snuggled under the covers feeling safer than she'd felt for a long time.

~*~

The next morning Rebecca donned the dress. It was loose on her but would suffice.

"Looks like we need to fatten you up, Rebecca," Erin commented. "Let's go to the dining area, I'm famished."

"You're not sea sick?" questioned Rebecca.

"No, are you? You look a little green."

"I feel better than last night. I think I can eat something." She hoped that her queasiness was due to her previous over-indulgence. After all her stomach was not used to so much food.

The girls went to the dining area where others were eating. There were women in beautiful traveling gowns and men in fine frocked coats. Rebecca immediately felt out of place, but Erin sat down at a table and began to converse with an older couple. Rebecca joined them but kept her eyes on her hands in front of her. She looked at them and quickly hid them in her lap. They did not look like the hands of one who would be traveling in a cabin. They were worn and rough, and her fingernails were broken from hard work.

Soon the couple knew Erin's reasons for sailing to America, and they shared theirs, "We are on our way to America to start a church in the west. We have heard that there are few churches and even fewer preachers. We hope to make a difference and maybe see a few Indians come to know the Lord, as well."

The couple turned their attention to Rebecca, "My dear, you look poorly. You're so thin and your face is bruised. Are you okay?"

Erin looked at her traveling companion and for the first time noticed what had been so obvious to the couple.

Rebecca faltered, "I...I...have been sick, and last night I fell. I'm fine now. I...seem to be gaining my strength back slowly." Rebecca hated to lie about her bruises, but long ago became conditioned to conceal the truth about her "accidents."

"Well, dear, if you need anything, just look for us."

"Thank you...I...I...will."

The others turned their attention back to their conversation of the west, and although Rebecca did not understand all that the three talked about, she listened attentively to their conversation and envied their joy and excitement for the future.

They were served hot cakes and bacon. Rebecca had never seen anything so delicious as the meal set before her. It was a far cry from the porridge she was given to eat each morning at home. Hesitant after yesterday's over-indulgence, she ate slowly and stopped before she was full.

~*~

Afterwards, when the breakfast was cleared and the passengers had gone on deck, Erin was able to get her other belongings to Rebecca's cabin without notice. Once back out on deck with the other passengers, Rebecca felt relieved that no one had noticed the switch.

"Rebecca," Erin asked, "What story are we going to tell others? Are we sisters? Best friends? Twins?" Erin giggled with the thought. They didn't think they looked at all alike, so they couldn't pass as sisters. They decided that they would tell others that they were best friends traveling together.

Everywhere about them were seamen working on their routine tasks. Rebecca marveled at all the work it took to keep the ship in good condition, men scraping and painting and a lot of activities she had no names for.

The girls stood at the railing, listening to the sea lapping the side of the ship, feeling the salt air on their faces, and breathing in all the freshness. Rebecca had never smelled anything as good as fresh air. She had not realized how stuffy her home and the shop had been until she was out here in the breeze.

A young man with blonde hair approached the two and said, "Erin."

Erin spun around and quickly recognized the young man, "Thomas Dooley! What are you doing here? I did not know you were going to America!"

"When I heard you were going I couldn't bear the thought of you leaving without me, so I booked a passage, too!"

"Oh, Thomas, you are such a flatterer."

"And who is your lovely companion," he said as he gazed on Rebecca with appreciative eyes.

Rebecca blushed at his obvious appraisal of her.

"This is my friend, Rebecca. We are traveling together.

Rebecca, this is my friend, Thomas Dooley. We grew up together. He always knew how to treat a girl right," she said with a chuckle and a twinkle in her eye.

"Nice to meet you, Rebecca," he said.

Rebecca nodded, "Nice to meet you, Mr. Dooley."

Turning his gaze back on Erin, he said with a laugh, "Erin, will you ever forget what I did to you in school?"

"I don't know. The memory of you chasing me with that frog still gives me nightmares," she said in feigned indignation.

"Please forgive me, my dear."

"And if I don't?"

"Well, then," looking around him, "I guess I will just have to show you my pet fish."

"Oh, no, I forgive you."

"Then prove it by taking a walk with me?"

"Rebecca? Would you like to take a walk with this scoundrel?" beamed Erin.

"We're on a ship with hundreds of people. We will stay on deck where they can all watch and make sure that I am a gentleman," he said bowing to the girls.

"No doubt it would take all two-hundred of them to make sure of that, and that's the truth of it," she smiled at him and took the arm that he offered and hooked the other arm in Rebecca's. Rebecca haltingly kept up with the two. They continued to reminisce, and although it would have been easy to feel like a third wheel, Erin kept Rebecca engaged in the conversation.

Later when Erin and Rebecca were back in the room alone, Erin started giggling and bubbled with joy, "Rebecca, can you believe it, he really did come on board because of me!"

She climbed up onto her bunk and hugged herself, "I have always liked him, and when he decided to become a minister, I was afraid that he would run off with someone more fitting than me."

Rebecca became worried for her friend. Would she become another victim of marriage that her mother and she had become? Rebecca shuddered at the memory of her wedding night.

"What's the matter, Rebecca? You look as if you've seen a ghost."

Rebecca wanted to keep her past hidden from Erin, but she needed to let it out. It was eating her alive, and she did not even know what she was going to do with herself when she got to America. Maybe Erin would be able to help her find a job or just tell her what to do.., and just maybe her story would convince Erin not to pursue this relationship with this man.

"Erin, marriage is awful. You don't want to marry anyone. I'm never getting married, again," Rebecca blurted out.

"Again?"

For the first time since Rebecca had met Erin, she seemed to be speechless as she listened to Rebecca's tale of her wedding day and subsequent boarding of the ship.

Finally, when Rebecca was finished, Erin sobbed, "Oh, you poor, poor dear. I'm so sorry." She climbed down from her bunk and went over to the weeping young girl and held her.

After some time, Erin said, "Rebecca, not all men are like your papa and your...umm....husband. My papa never laid a hand on me, and I know that Thomas would not either. His family is the most gentle, happy family I have ever met. Honest!"

It was hard for Rebecca to believe Erin, but she just nodded her head in acceptance of what Erin had said.

"Rebecca worried aloud, "I have no idea what to do when I get to America, but I could not go back to my home, and I could not stay with that man. I was afraid I would get arrested!"

"Arrested? For what?"

"For killing him."

Erin laughed, "Honey, you didn't kill him! No doubt all that exercise he was getting did it or maybe the Good Lord saw fit to help you escape him!"

The Good Lord? Rebecca wondered, did she mean God? Maybe someone else could see that He was a part of the plan for her to escape her father.

Rebecca shuddered at the thought of the man she had called husband so briefly and sighed, "But what am I to do now?"

"*Hmmmm*, I'm sure we can figure it out. Maybe Thomas can help us."

"No!" Rebecca shrieked in fear, "You have to promise me that you won't tell a soul!"

Erin looked at her with surprise at her outburst and agreed not to tell Thomas.

The days passed without a solution to Rebecca's problem. They continued to meet Thomas on deck for walks, play games, or sit with other passengers and listen to stories of America. Many were following family that had gone before them. A few of them brought out their instruments and played, as others danced. Once a whole family came and acted out a play. It was quite humorous, and Rebecca found herself laughing. It felt good to do that. They had been having a peaceful voyage and for that Rebecca was grateful.

Chapter 5

The third week of the voyage began with a darkness that seemed to permeate Rebecca's very soul. Huge waves were beating against the ship, and Rebecca clung to the railing. Seamen were running everywhere as they prepared for a storm.

Thomas joined the pair and said, "The captain says we're in for a big one."

He could barely be heard above the clapping of the sails overhead and the calls of the seamen as they barked orders to each other.

Rebecca jumped as lightning flashed across the sky in front of her. The threesome couldn't keep their eyes off of the waves as they grew larger and their crests broke in white foam against the ship.

A seaman broke their concentration when he bellowed out a warning to the passengers to go to their cabins or to steerage below. As they turned to go, large drops of rain splashed all about them, and they were drenched before they were able to gain cover. The seamen warned them not to light lanterns as it got darker for fear of starting a fire if they were knocked over. Once those from steerage were below, the seamen latched the door giving them no light at all.

The ship pitched and rolled, and it was not easy to walk. Rebecca held onto the wall to keep from falling and to find her way to the cabin. She quickly unlocked the cabin door and burst inside as the ship pitched a different way. She gasped as she struggled to gain her footing. She finally made it to the bunk and climbed on top. Erin and Thomas were right behind her and sat down on the opposite berth.

They immediately began to pray for their safety and that the storm would pass. It was in awe that Rebecca noticed that the storm grew gradually weaker until she did not hear thunder anymore. She sighed with relief and was beginning to think twice about the power of prayer and even more in Erin and Thomas's trust in this Someone they could not see.

~*~

The fourth week found Erin seeking Rebecca out to announce to her, "Thomas and I are getting married as soon as we get to America. He has family in New York City, and they need a church. Isn't it wonderful?"

Rebecca smiled at her friend. She was still unsure if marriage was such a good idea, but she couldn't help joining in the girl's joy. She too had enjoyed Thomas's company, and he had always treated her like a lady.

"And I figured out what you can do, too! You can take my tickets and go in my place to my brother's! His wife seems wonderful, and I bet he wouldn't care who came, as long as he had help!"

Rebecca pondered the offer and realized she had not much of a choice. She could not be wandering the streets of America all alone.

"Are you sure he won't mind?"

"My brother is a fine man, and he and his wife would welcome you and your help!"

Rebecca reluctantly agreed. Erin had convinced her that she needed to tell Thomas about their arrangement. They needed his help to get Rebecca off the ship and onto the right trains. But Rebecca did not want anyone to know the reasons for her leaving her home country. She made Erin promise to tell Thomas only the necessary information.

Erin told Thomas that Rebecca was coming to America to find work. She told him that both Rebecca and she had agreed that the best place to do that was to go to Austin's.

Thomas was glad that Rebecca was willing to fulfill Erin's commitment to her brother. He did not like the idea of leaving Austin and his wife stranded, nor allowing his future wife to use the tickets to fulfill the commitment she made to receive them. He did tell Erin that he would send Austin the money for the passage across the ocean.

So it was settled. Whether Rebecca wanted to or not, her future had been decided. She hoped that if she was truly in God's hands that this was His plan for her life.

~*~

One morning found the passengers abuzz with excitement. Another ship was spotted ahead on its way to Europe. The passengers were scrambling to find paper and pens to write letters to their loved ones in hopes that they could pass the letters on to the oncoming ship. Erin was caught up in the excitement, too. She found what she needed and began to write to her family about her upcoming nuptials. Then she paused and looked up at Rebecca, "You could write to your mother!"

Rebecca lamented, "My father would never give it to her."

"Don't you know someone you could send it to that would give it to her?"

"Why yes I do!" Rebecca remembered the praying lady and knew she was the perfect choice. Erin handed her the paper and pen and ink. Rebecca didn't hesitate but started writing. She told her mother that she missed her, that she was on her way to America, and that she had a job. She didn't know what to say about her husband. She finally said simply that he died in his sleep.

The two ships got as close as they could and the seamen passed the letters over. A cheer went up when the letters made it safely to the other ship. Rebecca found herself saying a little prayer that it would make it safely into the right hands.

~*~

Two weeks later, the weary travelers arrived safely in America. Thomas's family met them at the docks and once they saw Rebecca and Erin with him they gave them warm greetings. Thomas's uncle, Timothy Dooley, was a doctor and had brought his young bride, Elizabeth, to America fifteen years earlier. Thomas introduced his family to Erin, his future bride.

"We plan to marry here and work together in the church," he added.

Elizabeth exclaimed with glee, "Oh, a wedding. I so love weddings. Do you have a family in New York City, Erin?"

"No, I don't. My brother lives on the prairie, though."

"Please then allow us the honor of giving you a wedding."

Thomas turned to Rebecca, thus far neglected in the news of the wedding, "This is Erin's friend, Rebecca O'Neal. She will be traveling on to help Erin's brother with his family."

"Rebecca, it is nice to meet you. You must stay with us until the wedding."

Erin turned to Rebecca with excitement in her voice, "Oh, Rebecca, I would love to have you be a part of my wedding. It would make me so happy. You're the only girl I know here in America. Please stay until then."

Rebecca hesitated for a moment, but the look in Erin's eyes told her that she could not say no to this simple request of her friend who had practically rescued her on the ship.

She nodded her head and smiled at Erin. Erin squealed and hugged her dear friend.

"Now, ladies, we need to make our way to our home. We cannot stay out here making wedding plans in the middle of the wharf," commanded Dr. Dooley. The women obediently turned and boarded the waiting carriage.

Rebecca stood in awe before the beautiful brownstone house of the Dooley's. But she was even more amazed when she entered the house. They were immediately greeted by a servant who took their belongings and delivered them to their rooms.

They had walked into an entrance way that was bigger than her living area at home. The two girls were escorted up the spiral staircase to a room with two beds. Erin and Rebecca would share the room. It was so bright and cheery, Rebecca couldn't help but feeling cheerful herself.

Elizabeth said, as she seemed to flow into the room behind them, "I'm sorry that the room is so small. We have other guests this evening. I'll leave you to bathe and rest. The maid will be up to help you with your bath. Someone will bring you a tray of light snacks to nibble on until dinner. Dinner is at six o'clock. Have a nice rest." She smiled and shut the door behind her as she exited.

Rebecca stared after her. Was she in a dream? She had never been treated so royally before. Erin giggled and Rebecca spun around.

"It's beautiful, isn't it?"

"Yes, I've never seen a house like this," Rebecca said gazing at the paintings on the wall, the carpet, and the matching beds.

As promised, a maid came in to help them with their baths. Rebecca was embarrassed to have the young girl wait on her. The girl did not seem to notice her uneasiness and once the girls had soaked and bathed she helped them dress into soft cotton nightgowns that Elizabeth had provided.

Erin seemed to enjoy all the pampering, but Rebecca felt odd and so very unworthy of the attention.

The girls crawled under cool sheets and the drapes were drawn. Rebecca thought over the last hour of her travel and wanted to pinch herself to see if it was all real. She did not deserve any attention but did not know how to stop it. Her eye lids were growing heavier and so she closed her eyes to the splendor around her and soon dozed.

After the girls dressed for dinner they walked down the staircase to join the rest of the family waiting for them. Rebecca thought that her bedroom was beautiful but upon entering the dining room she gasped at its beauty. A huge chandelier glistened above the table that was decorated in pure white linen, vases of fresh cut flowers, shiny silver serving bowls, crystal glasses, and colorful China pieces.

Rebecca stood just inside the doorway with her mouth open in surprise. Mrs. Dooley rose to greet the girls and led them to high backed tapestry seats. Rebecca sat down and remained silent throughout the meal. The others seemed to sense her aloofness and took it for fatigue.

Plates full of chicken, roasted potatoes, steaming vegetables, and warm rolls were passed to the visitors. Rebecca ate slowly, not wanting to show poor manners. She watched Mrs. Dooley and followed her suit.

Rebecca did not need to worry about joining in the conversation. Thomas was relaying his story about Erin and their childhood, his following her onto the ship, and courting her there. Erin put in a few words here and there but Rebecca could tell that she was a little nervous and not her normal talkative self.

Rebecca observed the interaction of the family. The doctor smiled at his wife and reached over and touched her arm often throughout the meal. Rebecca sat with awe at the relationship the couple displayed. Was it real? She had never seen her father touch her mother except in anger.

Rebecca and Erin spent several days resting and working on getting healthy. The trip had tired Erin out and the Dooleys were concerned about her. But their major concern was over Rebecca.

At first glance at Rebecca, Dr. Dooley had become concerned about her thin form. He told her that she could not leave until she had gained some strength. Dr. Dooley wanted to examine her, but she promised that she would be feeling better once she had some rest so the doctor did not press her but kept an eye on her. She was determined to get his permission to leave and fought through the fatigue and made sure in his presence that she appeared well. A little rouge on her cheeks helped with that as well.

~*~

Rebecca continued to watch this family interact. She marveled at the way they treated each other. There was never a harsh word. She had never seen a man that did not raise his voice or his hand to his wife. Maybe he does in the privacy of their bed chamber. If so, would there not be bruises? She continued to watch them and came to the conclusion they were truly a unique family. Maybe Erin had been right about Thomas. It was obvious that his family were good to each other.

Chapter 6

Austin yelled, "Whoa!" and the work horse stopped. He dropped the reigns for a moment and readjusted the harness on his back. He looked over at the children sitting quietly along the edge of the field. The baby gave out a lusty cry, no doubt out of hunger. Austin sighed as he called to the girls who seemed to ignore their brother's complaints.

"Feed the baby, girls. He's hungry."

"But, Papa, he stinks," exclaimed the girls as they held their noses and giggled at how silly each other looked. Austin groaned, released himself from the harness, and walked the rows to where the children were. He had brought all the supplies that he needed to take care of the children in the field: diapers, wet rags, milk, and a lunch.

He hastily changed the boy. "I am getting used to this," he remarked dryly. He looked at the little guy. He'd been so busy that he never really looked at him. In all honesty, he had never even said the child's name out loud. He paused to look at his sweet innocent face and said, "Hello, Ryan Austin

Finnigan. I'm your papa. You've had a rough beginning, but I promise you that it will get better. Soon your Auntie Erin will be here. She'll make everything better."

The girls had been standing nearby watching their dad. They came and clung to him, needing the same reassurance that everything would be okay. Austin looked at them. They were dirty, and their hair was a mess. Victoria would not have been happy if she saw them. He mustered a smile and said, "Yes, when your aunt comes things will get better. Come on, girls, let's get some lunch."

He escorted the children down to the creek where he washed up and then began pulling out the food from the basket. He was grateful that Mrs. White had continued to provide bread for his family. He cut each child a chunk of it along with a piece of cold ham and a cup full of milk. He kept the milk and meat cool while in the fields by placing them in the creek. The girls chattered on about pretend houses in the root of the tree and furniture of burrs and tables made from flowers. He looked at them quizzically. They dragged him to the tree near the field. They had quite a menagerie. They had set up a pretend home right there in the tree roots. He smiled at their ingenuity. He yearned to give them the life only a mother could give. He gave them each a pat on the head, got Ryan settled and returned to his work. Though he tried to focus on his fields, he could not block out his thoughts, thoughts of Victoria or his predicament.

He was exhausted. The baby woke him through the night, the children needed his attention, and the fields had to be worked. He did not know how long he could go on. He was counting on one thing, that his sister would arrive soon. He had known that with a fourth child, even Victoria could not continue as she had, and so he sent his sister tickets for a passage across the ocean and train tickets to bring her to their family. Now, more than ever, he was grateful that he had sent for her. Surely she would arrive soon.

~*~

When Erin and Rebecca were up to it, they began planning for the wedding and Rebecca's trip out west. With the money from her husband Rebecca was able to purchase a traveling dress and some under garments. For the wedding Rebecca would wear another one of Erin's gowns. Elizabeth had her own wedding dress refitted for Erin.

The day of the wedding found Erin chattering even more than usual. Rebecca stood to the side and envied her only friend. She was so happy and so in love with Thomas. Rebecca hoped that she could someday have someone that loved her as much as Thomas loved Erin. The wedding was beautiful and Erin glowed. It was a joyous day shared with friends and family.

A few days later Rebecca insisted it was time for her to begin her journey across America. Dr. Dooley had grown quite fond of her and said, "Rebecca, I wish that you were not leaving yet. When you first came from the ship, I was concerned that you would not even make it to our home. You do look so much healthier today, but I think that you should stay here and get even stronger."

"Dr. Dooley, you have been so good to me. These few days in your home have helped me recover from my long trip, Rebecca replied, "But I must go. Erin's brother and his wife need me. Their baby may have already come. I cannot stay a moment longer." Of course, on the inside, Rebecca wished that she could have stayed there and not traveled into another unknown. She had enjoyed her days at the Dooley's. She had not told the doctor about the true reason behind her poor health and was hesitant to divulge such facts. Yes, it was true, the outer scars and bruises had healed but there were far greater ones, the inner ones that remained. However, she knew she had a responsibility to Erin's brother.

"If you find that when you reach the prairie, you do not like it or are no longer needed, you are welcome in our home," Dr. Dooley insisted.

Rebecca was surprised at his offer and graciously thanked him.

At the train station, Thomas set the satchel filled with Rebecca's few belongings down on the platform as Erin hugged her and gave her the long strip of tickets. Rebecca looked smart in her dark traveling dress with matching black straw hat. She had never worn anything so becoming before. The pair had trouble conversing as the train noisily approached the station. Rebecca turned to look at the huge contraption that would be carrying her into the unknown. Smoke billowed out of the stack, and the platform shook as the train approached and then stopped.

Above the ruckus Erin gave Rebecca last minute instructions, "You'll be changing trains a lot. But just show them your tickets and they'll direct you to the right place. Do you remember where you're going?"

"Yes, Kingston, Iowa," Rebecca said slowly and clearly.

Erin encouraged Rebecca to write to her and gave her a note for her brother to read with the money from the passage Thomas had promised.

Rebecca clung to the only true friend that she had ever had and remembered her earlier parting from her mother. Tears formed in her eyes at the loss of her mother and now her friend. Would she ever find the love that she sought? Erin smiled at her, "It'll be okay. You're in God's hands! And that's for sure!"

"Time to board, ma'am," a man in a dark suit and cap announced. "Is that your satchel?" Rebecca looked at him warily and stepped back as if in fear.

Erin rescued her and answered him, "Yes it is, thank you." He took the satchel and helped Rebecca to climb up into the last car. Rebecca glanced back at Erin and Thomas as they waved to her. She followed the man through the door of the car and walked between two rows of red velvet seats full of people. She was surprised at how bright the little car was. She noticed that the sides of the car were almost completely made of windows.

Rebecca sat down on one of the seats that the man showed her and quickly turned her gaze to outside and found Erin and Thomas still watching for her. The engine whistled, and the train jerked, jolting Rebecca back into her seat. It jerked again and then began to shake as Thomas and Erin began to wave to her again. She waved and continued to do so until they were only specks in the distance. The town quickly passed before her and eventually she turned her gaze downward. Tears filled her eyes at the complete loneliness that seemed to fill her. How she wished that she had stayed behind with Erin. But how could she? Erin was married now and would be going with her husband to start a new life together. In God's hands, Erin had said. Yes, she had to believe that she was in God's hands or the fear would overwhelm her and consume her.

Her thoughts turned to her last few words with the doctor. She had never met anyone like him. The whole time she was at his home she expected to be treated abusively or at least be expected to work for her keep, but he had asked nothing from her. She could not understand his total acceptance of her. So she registered it with the other experiences she had in the world outside of the little shop in Ireland and began hoping that the world was not as altogether dark and dreary as she once assumed.

Sometime later, a man came into the car wearing a dark suit with brass buttons. He wore a cap with the letters *CONDUCTOR* etched across the front. He stopped and talked to each passenger and collected the tickets.

Rebecca fumbled in her purse and pulled out the long strip of tickets. The conductor smiled at her and tore off the parts that he needed and gave the rest back. She quickly placed the remaining tickets back into the purse and turned her gaze back to the ever-changing landscape passing before her eyes.

Her thoughts turned to the thing that was ever present in her mind. What did the future hold for her? She felt uneasy about meeting strangers and announcing that she was Erin's replacement. What if they didn't like her? What if they didn't need her anymore? What if the husband was as cruel as her own father? Her heart beat quickened at the thought of being homeless. Did she have enough money left over from her husband to take care of herself until she could find employment? And what skill could she perform? She did know how to do figures and keep track of the stock at her father's shop. Would that be enough to find her a job? She remembered that she had been offered a place in the doctor's home, if she desired, but she felt uneasy about that option. After all, they may have just been trying to be friendly.

She looked around at her fellow travelers. She spotted a happy family traveling together. A tear came to her eye. Would she ever be happy? This family did not seem anything like her own. They made it seem possible for one to be happy. She closed her eyes as if to guard herself from the truth. She was alone, with no one to love or to love her. In the midst of her worry she remembered Erin's words, "In God's hands." She was in God's hands. He had brought her this far. He would take care of her. She tried to rest in that hope.

The days became a blur. She would leave one train to board another. There was always someone to direct her to the next train. She spent hours sitting in train stations in towns she did not know. She wished each stop would be the last. The string of tickets diminished until the final one remained.

~*~

At one point Rebecca got off the train and was directed with other immigrants to the Emigrant House. She stood among the hundred people and watched the uniformed man with a list in his hand read name after name from the list of those preparing to ride the Union Pacific train. Once a name was called, the family would gather their belongings and run for one of the cars. Rebecca soon realized that the first car was only for women and children.

Rebecca watched each family as it were called. Often the man barked out orders and reprimanded them for being so slow. Rebecca watched as his wrath was demonstrated several times on the poor immigrants who had trouble understanding his words. Rebecca grimaced at his harsh words as flashes of her father's face appeared before her. She realized that once again the Dooley's were an exception to the rule of how she saw men. Men were cruel and looked for weak women to abuse and destroy with their words. She shook off the desire to run and stood her ground, concentrating on the names that he called until she heard her name. Fighting back the hot tears, and with a determination not to allow another man to abuse her, she quickly gathered her meager belongings and marched past him, not giving him any opportunity to strike out at her.

Rebecca climbed the steps and entered the barely lit car. She waited for her eyes to adjust from brilliant light to darkness. She looked around and saw that there was little seating in the car. This train was much different than all the ones she rode in the east. It looked uncomfortable. The benches were short with barely enough room for her, let alone the older women surrounding her. She looked around for a place to sit and spied a woman wrestling with several children. The woman looked up at her and smiled, "I noticed you be traveling alone. If you help me with the children I can offer you some companionship and some of my food."

Tired of the loneliness that seemed to cover her like a shroud since she left Erin and Thomas, Rebecca quickly agreed to the arrangement. She was tired of bringing attention to herself by traveling alone and sat down across from the woman. One of the little girls looked at Rebecca shyly, her fingers in her mouth. Rebecca leaned forward and talked softly to the child. In no time at all the little girl was on Rebecca's lap and sleeping soundly. Rebecca sighed. She had been worried about her ability to take care of children when she arrived at the Finnigan's. Well, if this little girl was any indication of what it was like to take care of children, she could do it. The woman gave her an encouraging smile.

The ride seemed to take forever, and the conditions were less than comfortable. They stopped twice a day to allow townspeople to board the train and sell food or to allow the passengers to get off and be served at a house nearby.

The first time the passengers were allowed to get off to go to a house nearby Rebecca and her traveling companions had barely been served when the call to re-board came. They scrambled from their seats, leaving behind half-eaten food in fear of being left behind.

At the next stop, Rebecca purchased food that could be carried and quickly returned to the car. She took the hardboiled egg, boiled potato in its skin, and the chunk of dark bread from the handkerchief she had wrapped them in. She ate the food quickly, but had trouble keeping it down and soon found herself retching.

The next day was much the same. She could not seem to keep anything in her stomach. That coupled with little sleep found her growing weaker each day. She longed to stop the shaking and the constant jostle of the train and sleep on solid ground again.

The woman that she sat with gave her a worried look as she ran to lose another meal again. Rebecca yearned to finally reach her destination. She was exhausted, and she was experiencing dizzy spells. If she wasn't so tired, she might have realized that something truly was wrong with her.

One day, the train stopped suddenly, and the children and women lurched forward. Coals from the stove flew out, and one of the children's dresses caught fire. Rebecca dived for the little girl, extinguishing the flames with her own body, but not before the fire had burned holes in her dress. The mother was so grateful. Rebecca looked at her dress and gasped. It was ruined, but she had no choice to continue to wear it. She wearily laid down on the bench someone had offered her, but rest did not come.

~*~

Mrs. White looked across the table to the weary Austin, "We missed you at church on Sunday."

Austin ignored her and drained his cup of coffee. He had no time for church. He had two jobs to fulfill daily, and it took all of his strength to do the necessities. "I have work to do. Thanks for the bread. We appreciate it," he said a little coldly.

She smiled at him and reached her hand out to him, "It'll be easier once your sister comes."

Her smile could usually melt him, but not this time. His bitterness was mounting, and the stress was showing. He stood up shrugging off her hand and called the children to go to the fields. They reluctantly obeyed and left Mrs. White sitting at the table.

She rose and washed up the stack of dishes in the sink, dusted and swept the rooms, and gathered up laundry that she would take with her and return to Austin the following day. At the door she turned and sighed, "Oh, Lord, Austin needs a miracle, and it seems like he's not talking to Thee much these days. So I'm coming to Thee on his behalf. Send his sister quickly or provide a solution that we can all live with."

She sighed and looked over the house as she stood in the doorway. It needed so much attention, but she could not give anymore and so reluctantly turned and left.

Diana Barclay

Chapter 7

After several days that seemed like weeks in Rebecca's weakened state, she arrived at her destination exhausted. She had heard Kingston, Iowa, being called and wearily picked up her satchel, smiled good-bye at the woman she had helped, and disembarked. She stood there alone looking around her as the train made its way further onto its other destinations.

She was surprised at how small the little town was and inquired about Austin Finnigan at the general store. The clerk looked at her dirty singed clothes and chalky face.

"I'm sending out a delivery that way. My boy can drop you off at their place."

"I'd be much obliged," she said with relief flooding through her body. "Just a little while longer, and I can rest," she said to herself as if to push onward.

She was so weary that she did not give much more than a glance to the little town. It was so tiny Rebecca wondered how she would find employment there if she was turned away at the Finnigan's.

The boy came with the wagon, and Rebecca climbed aboard and sat beside him. She was grateful that he was not one for talking, because she barely had enough strength to get to the farm and offer her assistance to the new mother and family.

The wagon lurched forward, and Rebecca held on to keep from falling over. It was as if she was willing herself to hold on just a little while longer.

"Here we are," announced the boy. Rebecca looked up from nodding off to see a wooden structure not much bigger than her own home back in Ireland.

The boy called out and a tall man holding a baby in his arms emerged from the house. She thought how odd it looked to see the baby in the big muscular arms of the man.

The boy helped Rebecca down from the wagon, and she nervously looked at the man. She pulled herself up to her full height and hoped that she did not look as weak as she felt. If she was to hire on here, she'd have to prove that she could do the work.

"Mr. Finnigan?" she asked.

He shook his head, yes, at the snip of a girl before him and waited patiently for her to go on. He looked at her hair that had come loose from its fastens, her dark sullen eyes, and her singed clothing and wondered what she was doing there.

"My name is Rebecca O'Don...I mean O'Neal. Your sister Erin sent me."

"Erin? Is she alright?"

"Yes, sir, in fact, she's married and living in New York City."

"But, I thought she was coming to help us."

"She sent me instead. She thought that I could be a help to your wife with all of your little ones. I have a letter for you from her," she smiled at the girls hiding behind their father's long legs.

Rebecca leaned against the wagon for support and hoped that she could finish this conversation.

"My wife...my wife is dead. So, you see, it would be inappropriate for me to hire you on. I was truly hoping for my sister to be here," he said as his own strength seemed to seep out. He had been holding on until his sister would be there.

Rebecca, realizing the gravity of his words, panicked. Where would she go? She had thought of the possibility of being turned away, but had not made any real plans if that would occur. She had been too sick and too weary to think beyond this moment. Now that the moment had arrived fear and helplessness overwhelmed her. She wavered and reached out to grip the wagon but lost her footing and strength and collapsed at Austin's feet.

~*~

Austin reacted quickly, handing the baby to one of the twins and picking Rebecca up, telling the boy to ride to the next farm and ask for Mrs. White to come at once. He carried the girl into the house surprised that she was so light and placed her on his bed.

Mrs. White arrived some time later. The girl had not moved at all, and Austin's worries showed on his face.

"Where did she come from?" Mrs. White asked as she looked at the girl. Her eyes quickly took in the sight before her. The girl wore a scorched, dusty dress. Her eyes were sunken with dark circles. She was thin, dangerously thin. Her face was pale.

"Back east, I suppose. Y'know my sister was to come help us, but she stayed in the east and sent me this girl. That's all I know about her."

"What's her name?"

"Rebecca. Rebecca O'Neal. Will she be alright?"

"I don't know. Go into the other room so that I can examine her."

Austin left the room with a worried look. The girl had not even stirred since he had carried her into the room.

The children were sitting in the main room quietly, their eyes big with worry.

"Papa, is the girl going to be okay?" asked Kelly Anne.

"I don't know."

Austin sat down in the rocker and the children joined him.

~*~

After examining her, Mrs. White walked out into the living area and said, "Austin, she's dehydrated, malnourished, and exhausted."

"Will she get better?" he asked.

"Yes, but that's not all. I believe that she is with child."

Surprised, Austin argued, "But she's only a child, herself."

"I would say that young girl has a story to tell when she is well and I'd imagine it will not be a happy one. Try to get her to drink and eat as much as you can."

Austin looked at her. Was she telling him to take care of the girl? His mind raced. He could not take on one more responsibility, "I cannot take care of her. Can't you take her to your house?"

"I have too many to take care of at my house now," she answered not unkindly.

"But, I can barely take care of my responsibilities. How can I take care of her?"

"The Good Lord has seen it fit to send her your way. He knows what He is doing. I will come over when I can and will send John Jr. over to help with the chores. You must take good care of her."

Austin knew from the few years of dealing with Mrs. White that there was no arguing. She left, and with shoulders slumped as if all the emotional weight he was carrying was too much for him, Austin retrieved some water from the pail and went into the bedroom. He looked down at the girl laying so still in the bed. He immediately gave her a spoonful of the cool water. She stirred but did not awaken.

Austin stared at her. She looked so young and so pale underneath the beautiful wedding ring quilt his wife had made for their bed. Austin stayed by the girl's side as much as possible the rest of that day and into the night. She roused only briefly for a few minutes where he tried quickly to get her to drink more of the water and sip some broth. She seemed so incoherent and restless. She cried out in fear and pain many times in her sleep. Austin grieved for the girl and the horror that must have been in her past.

He sensed that her struggles were deeper than just physical fatigue, and for the first time since his wife's death he retrieved the family Bible. Hoping to bring her some peace, he began reading to her from his favorite passages. Although he had meant to read the words for the girl's benefit, the Scriptures seemed to soften his own anger at God for his wife's death.

As he read the words of encouragement, peace, and hope, he began to return to a trust and faith in God. Kneeling before the unconscious girl, he released his anger and bitterness and felt peace flood his soul. Why had he neglected the very One who would give him peace?

Rebecca heard the deep voice speaking words of peace and love to her. It was as if the voice was calling her to come back. But she liked the dream world. She was at peace, and the words and the deep voice seemed to dance in her head lulling her deeper into herself.

~*~

By the third day Austin looked regrettably out the window toward his fields. Would he lose his crops? He had no choice but to stay by the girl's bedside plus take care of his baby and children. He saw a movement outside and rose from the chair and walked closer to the window to get a better look. He was surprised to see several of his neighbors working his field. He breathed a sigh of relief at the knowledge that his hard work would not be in vain.

Mrs. White returned on the fourth day to bring a supply of food and baked goods. She bathed the girl who seemed to respond little to anything around her. So she began speaking to the girl, "Rebecca, your baby needs you. Come back. Fight to get well. You are needed. Your baby needs you."

"Baby? What baby?" Rebecca asked the kind voice that she hoped was her mother's. She did not know if she had voiced her question or if it had just joined the other words floating in her mind. Then she remembered the baby in the man's arms. "Maybe, it's that baby." The thought that an innocent little baby could need her willed her to slowly fight her way through the fog. With it came the pain of remembering. But she was needed by someone that could not hurt her, and so she fought through. The words that the deep voice had read to her churned in her mind and gave her strength and in some way acted as a guide past the evil faces of her father and her husband until she opened her eyes to see another man's face above her.

She gasped and tried to move away from him. "It's okay, no one's going to hurt you here," Austin said softly.

It was the voice in her mind, and it brought peace to her troubled soul, and she relaxed.

"Here, drink some broth. It will make you strong."

She obeyed, never taking her eyes from the green ones that seemed to see through into her soul. She closed her eyes again, "Oh, so tired, but the baby needs me," she whispered as her lips curled up into a slight smile.

The next time she awoke it was to three sets of little girls' eyes. She smiled at them and tried to reach for them, but they scampered away giggling calling, "Papa, Papa, she's awake."

The man entered the room again with a tray and smiled at her. She had never seen a man smile at her in that way, only the young boy that visited her at the store, but he had been just a child, and she had assumed that once he became a man, he too, would become like her father.

"How are you feeling?" he asked in that deep voice that she had begun to associate with the feeling of peace and safety.

"Thirsty and hungry," she said shyly.

"That's good news," he said with a smile. She could not help but return one to him.

"Here, I'll help you sit up," he placed the tray down and went to help her. With the reflex of many years, Rebecca, at Austin's sudden movement, put her hands in front of her face and cowered in the bed.

Austin gasped and backed away from her. Remorse filled his being at the thought of what this girl had been through. "It's okay," he said quietly. "I'm not going to hurt you."

She lowered her hands and eyed him cautiously, and then on her own, she sat up.

"Here's a pillow for behind you."

She leaned forward for him to place the pillow, not convinced that it was not a trick. Her father had played tricks on her as a child until she learned not to trust his lies. He, too, had acted like he was helping her and then, just as she thought he was going to treat her right, he would slap or punch her and laugh at her for being so stupid.

Austin quickly placed the pillow behind her, noticing the tensing of her muscles, and then he stepped back away from her to show her that he meant her no harm.

"Where's the baby?" She asked him as she ate from the tray he had given her. She did not remove her dark blue eyes from his strong face, ready at a moment to protect herself. "He needs me."

"He's in the next room. Do you want me to go get him?"

She nodded and watched him as he left the room and returned with the infant. She put the tray aside and reached for the child. Austin gently laid his son in her arms and watched as tears came to her eyes. She caressed his face and looked at his tiny hands. "He's so helpless. He really does need me," she said more as a question than a statement.

Austin was unsure of what to say and felt it wouldn't hurt for her to think that she was needed, "Yes, he needs you. He needs you to get well."

With a childlike determination she looked up at the child's father, "He needs me. I need to get well."

Noticing that she was tiring, Austin offered to take the baby, and Rebecca held him up reluctantly. Feeling fatigue wash through her, she nestled back down in to the cool soft quilt and closed her eyes with an image of the tiny hands and face of the baby.

Rebecca seemed to be tuned into the baby's cries, and when he cried she awoke. Austin noticed her response and began bringing the baby in for the young girl to hold and feed. Rebecca grew stronger each day, determined to get well and take care of the baby.

The little girls became less and less shy as they stayed longer at her bedside. Rebecca smiled at them and soon they were climbing up on the bed to hug her and sit with her during the times she was awake. Rebecca had never known what it felt to be hugged so often, and she grew to eagerly anticipate the times when the girls told her stories and talked incessantly.

Mrs. White came to visit again and sat down beside Rebecca's bed. "When are you due, child?" she asked the girl.

"Do? I don't do anything much yet. Just take care of the baby when Mr. Finnigan brings him to me."

"No, dear, I mean when is 'your' baby coming?"

"My baby? That's my baby," pointing to the little boy asleep beside her.

"Honey, don't you know that there's a baby growing inside of you?"

Rebecca grasped her stomach and gasped at the size of it. She knew when women back home were going to have children because her mother had told her the baby was growing in their tummy. Her mother had not seen fit to explain much else to her, and not being raised on a farm around nature, she had no idea what it all meant.

"A baby is growing inside of me?" asked Rebecca.

"Yes, dear, do you know when the baby will be coming?"

"I don't know. How do you know?"

Mrs. White, surprised at the girl's ignorance, tried to explain to her the facts of life, "Do you have a husband? Are you married?"

"Yes, I...I.... My husband is dead."

"Well, dear, that baby inside of you is from your husband."

Rebecca gasped at the knowledge that Mr. O'Neal was responsible for this life growing inside of her. At the thought of him, she felt queasy and dizzy. The memory of his hot breath on her face and his rough ways came back to her. She buried her head in her hands and wept.

Mrs. White moved to sit beside her on the bed and crooned soft words to her until the crying subsided. "Tell me, Rebecca, what happened to you."

Rebecca, remembering the dead man she left in the hotel, panicked at the thought of telling someone the gruesome details. Even though Erin had told her it was not her fault she was still fearful of others finding it out.

Mrs. White pulled Rebecca close to her bosom and caressed her hair and continued to speak words of encouragement, "You can tell me, dear. I won't breathe a word to anyone. I swear!"

Rebecca looked at the woman who reminded her so much of her mother and in halting words spoke, "I got married and on our wedding night he died. He was planning on bringing me to America," Rebecca realized that she was leaving out a considerable amount of truth, but chose to only tell the necessary facts, "And so not having anywhere else to go I boarded the ship and came. I did not know I was going to have a baby."

Austin, in the next room, could not pull himself away from the doorway. "She's so young," he thought, "and has already seen so much tragedy in her short life. I can't imagine losing Victoria on our wedding night."

Once the story was out, Rebecca lay back as Mrs. White continued to speak softly to her. Rebecca closed her eyes and slept. Eventually, Mrs. White joined Austin in the next room, and realizing that he had heard her story said, "Austin, what are we going to do? She is so young and cannot be sent away. She has a baby to take care of, and she'll be weak for a while."

Austin looked up at her, shaking his head sadly, "I don't know."

"Well, I know. She needs you and you need a mother for your children. You told me of her nightmares. There is more to this child then she is letting on. You need to marry her. "

81

Austin looked at her in surprise, "Victoria has only been in the grave two months!"

"I told you before that the Good Lord brought this girl to you for a reason. I don't believe that it is just for her well-being only, but yours, as well. But, she cannot stay in your home very long before the neighbors will begin to talk."

"Couldn't she stay with you?" he asked knowing her answer before it was formed on her lips.

"I have my own family to take care of. We've no more room, and besides, she feels safe here, you can't send her away."

"No, no, it's too soon, and she doesn't feel safe around me." cried Austin.

"In time she will. You pray about it, Austin. I'll return in a few days for your answer."

Austin tried to think about the situation, but every time he did Victoria's face would be all he could see. How could he marry another woman when his loss was still so great? How could he commit himself to another woman when all he wanted was Victoria? It was too much to ask. He wanted to scream that at God. But instead he continued the routine of taking care of the girl and the children, numb from Mrs. White's words and what he knew to be the inevitable.

Chapter 8

The next day Rebecca was able to walk out to the other room, sit in the rocker, and even join the family for the evening meal. Austin had prepared johnnycakes and bacon along with Mrs. White's fresh bread. Rebecca ate heartily for the first time since she left New York. She was surprised at the abundance of food on the table. It reminded her of staying at the doctor's home. She did not think people in the west had so much to eat. The food at home had been so meager, she just assumed everyone else ate that way.

Austin watched her as she looked around the table, "Rebecca, eat what you want. There's plenty more."

She looked at Austin as he picked up the plate of johnnycakes and handed them to her.

"I wish we had something else, but this is about all I know how to make," he said with a chuckle.

Christie chimed in, "Mama made good food. I miss her cooking."

Austin had a faraway look in his eyes, "Me too, honey, me too."

Rebecca ate until she thought she would burst and looked up at Austin grinning at her. "The best way to get your strength back is to eat all that you want. You need to get strong for that baby of yours and for yourself."

Rebecca looked down at the plate shyly. Why was he so concerned about her, a stranger? Well, if she was going to stay here and work, she'd better earn her keep. She picked up her plate and the others on the table and carried them to the sink. She spotted an apron hanging on a peg and took it. It practically wrapped itself around her thin body twice. Austin's face turned white at the sight of his wife's apron around her, but he quickly gained composure as she began washing the dishes. Austin came over to her, "Are you sure you're strong enough to do that?"

Without looking at him, she said softly, "I...I'm okay. I can do them."

"Well, if you get tired, please stop. I don't want you getting sick again!" Austin turned and carried the baby to the other room and helped the children get ready for bed.

. ~*~

The next morning Rebecca awoke feeling stronger than the day before. She walked out to the kitchen to find Austin holding the baby and trying to fix breakfast. The baby was crying, and Rebecca went over to him and took him from Austin. He looked at her gratefully. She fed the baby and placed him on a blanket. The girls wakened and their chatter filled the quiet kitchen. Austin leaned down and gave each girl a hug and a kiss. Rebecca stared at him as he showed the girls such love. Austin looked up at her and smiled the same smile he had given his girls as they had entered the room. Rebecca looked away shyly and began to set the table.

Her mind was full of questions about this man. Maybe she was wrong about the Dooley's being unique. But this was not like her life in Ireland. Her father had not even given her a grunt of acknowledgment when she entered a room and he usually had a command of some kind for her to perform. She never would have found her father at the stove fixing supper. The thought of that was so inconceivable that Rebecca could not even picture it. She and her mother had waited on him for everything. He sat as a king in their home, barking out orders and letting both women know that they could not do anything right and that they were lucky that he allowed them in his sight. He often threatened to throw them both out on the street if they didn't do what he wanted perfectly. Both mother and daughter walked in fear daily.

With the table set and the food ready, Austin placed a steaming bowl of cornmeal on the table. He pulled out a chair and gestured to Rebecca to sit down. She obeyed, surprised at his gentlemanly ways. She had seen men in the shop who had opened the door for their wives and had escorted them into the shop. She had envied those women and desired to be treated the way they had.

She reached for one of the girl's plates to fill it, when she looked at Austin who had his head bowed. The girls did, too. She quickly put the plate down and followed their example. Austin's deep voice said simply, "Lord, thank Thee for providing this food for us today. May it strengthen us as we go about Thy will. Amen."

The sweet sound of "amen" echoed around the table as each of the girls followed their father's example. Rebecca said amen, as well, remembering how she had prayed at the table of Dr. Dooley.

Austin looked up at her and smiled, "You look better today. How do you feel?"

Rebecca did not look at him, grateful that she could concentrate on serving the girls their food, "I feel fine. Thank you."

"Do you think that you could take care of the children while I go out to the field? It's in sore need of attention. Our neighbors have done a fine job of keeping up with it, but they have fields of their own to tend."

"Yes, I can take care of the children."

To her surprise she heard the children cry out with glee, "Yea, Rebecca is going to take care of us!"

"Well, you girls mind Mrs. Rebecca and make sure she rests. Rebecca, if you need me, send one of the twins for me, and I'll come in immediately."

Austin shoveled the bowl of food down quickly. He could not cover his anxiousness to get to the fields. They seemed to have been calling him these past days during Rebecca's recovery. He loved to work in the fields. He loved the feel of the harness in his hands, the smell of the soil, the wind in his face, and the time alone to talk to His God. He had missed those days of being alone with Him. After Victoria had died, he had stopped talking to God. Now that he had made his peace, he was anxious to continue the close relationship that had been nourished in the hours so close to God's earth. Beyond that he needed alone time more than ever if he was to make a decision about Rebecca's future.

He took one last bite and got up from the table. He said his goodbyes to the girls and left the house with a bang of the door. Rebecca could not help noticing his desire to get to the fields. She saw the excitement in his eyes when she had told him that she could take care of the children. It brought a smile to her lips as it reminded her of the children's delight from a purchased surprise or a long saved for item in her old shop.

She rose from the table to watch Austin as he strode to the barn. She caught herself smiling as she noticed the spring in his step and heard his faint whistling. She envied him. He had been blessed with a purpose for his life. He seemed to know what he was meant to do and he enjoyed it. When she worked in the shop she enjoyed talking to the few customers that she had contact with, but she had never felt a joy about going to work.

She turned from the window to find the girls feeding the baby cornmeal. She ran to them and stopped them just as the spoon went to the baby's mouth. She shooed the girls off to their rooms to get dressed. She picked the baby up and snuggled him. How could you love someone so soon and so completely? She held him for a long time and then turned to the table, cleared it, and washed up the dishes.

Not used to so much exertion, she felt a little light headed and sat down in the rocker for a moment to catch her breath. She wanted to show Austin that she was worthy of her keep, however, so after a few minutes, she rose and preceded to help the children get dressed for the day. She was grateful when she found that the girls could take care of themselves with little prompting, and they even helped her change the baby.

~*~

Austin came back at lunchtime to make them a simple meal but to his surprise, found that Rebecca had already done so. He smiled at her and thanked her.

"Rebecca, you're looking tired. Has the morning been too much for you?"

"No," she said hesitantly, reviewing over the busy morning of keeping the girls out of trouble and settling squabbles.

"Well, you take a nap after lunch, and I'll take the children with me to the fields."

Rebecca did not answer but was grateful when Austin cleaned off the table after the meal and escorted the children out the door.

Rebecca went to her bed and slowly lowered herself to it, relieved at the chance to rest. She promised herself that she would rest for only a little while and then work on the supper meal. But she was still sleeping when Austin and the children returned.

She heard the children's chatter and jolted awake. Her heart began to beat quickly at the realization she had done something wrong. Embarrassed and frightened of the wrath that was surely to come, she walked out into the kitchen and started setting the table. She kept her head down, as she often did when she knew she had done something wrong. She had known that to look at her father would be a sign to him that she was impertinent and needed to be shown her place. She considered apologizing to Austin, but feared that would set him off into a rage, and so she decided to work silently.

Austin turned around and smiled at her, "You look rested. I was worried about you at lunch. I'm sorry that I left the children with you this morning."

The fear left her at his smile. She found herself drawn to it. She caught her breath and quickly put her head down and said quietly, "Really, I didn't mind. I enjoy their company."

"Well, we'll see how you feel tomorrow. You can't get overly tired. You need to rest and gain strength," he said with a worried look toward her. "You need to be strong for the birthing."

Rebecca blushed and said nothing.

Austin fixed another simple meal and retired early. The days of staying awake at night for Rebecca and the restless sleep he had when he did sleep was taking its toll.

Rebecca lay awake in bed for a while recounting the day. Austin was so considerate to her. She had done wrong, and he had not punished her for it. She smiled remembering his smiles. She gasped at the sudden thought that she just might do anything for another one. She vowed to get stronger and be a help to him, at least until it was time for her to leave. The sobering truth was that this job was only temporary. When would he send her away? The thought of leaving and trying to find a place to live frightened her. Now, with the baby coming, she knew she could not return to New York. The doctor had offered her a place to live, but she could not burden him with a child as well. She closed her eyes as tears formed. How was she going to survive? How was she going to take care of a baby?

In the next room, Austin lay listening to the sobbing from the bedroom. He wished that he could go to her and comfort her, but he had no words to offer. He lay awake long after the sobbing stopped, contemplating his dilemma. From the time of Victoria's death, he had assumed that his sister would arrive and take over the responsibility of the children. Why did she have to go and get herself married? Of course, he was sure that if she had known about Victoria's death, she would have come. Should he write to her and ask her to leave her new husband and fulfill her commitment to him? He knew that would not be the right thing to do. Erin had a new husband and a new life. His family was his responsibility. One thing he did know was that he could not go very much longer as father, mother, housekeeper, and farmer.

Could Mrs. White be right when she said that God had sent Rebecca to him? But how could he take another woman into his home as a substitute for Victoria? How could he love another? Why couldn't he have had Victoria instead?

Then an idea came to his mind. Couldn't he marry this woman in name only? After all, she was not ready for anything more. She seemed to have been hurt for so long in the past. But would a "business" contract marriage be fair to her? He would be asking far more from her than she was from him. These mangled thoughts that swirled in his mind.

"Oh, Victoria, why did you have to leave me?" he cried into his pillow.

~*~

Rebecca was greeted by a solemn Austin the next morning. He gave her a slight smile, but she sensed that he was deep in thought, and he did not look very rested. She helped him prepare breakfast in a silence that was finally broken by the children entering the room.

After praying and serving the children, Austin asked, "How are you feeling today, Rebecca?"

"I seem to feel stronger every day. I think I can take care of the children today." She was unsure of the truth behind those words, but she felt that she had to carry her load.

"Well, let's see how it goes this morning, and we can decide about the afternoon after lunch. Okay?"

Rebecca nodded and continued eating her porridge.

The morning went better than the day before. Rebecca found that it was best to give the girls something to do. She sent them out on the porch to play and entertain themselves. They even taught her a few games that they had learned from their mother, and soon the morning was over with Austin's arrival for lunch.

He stopped at the cold cellar and called Rebecca over to show her what was stored there. They took out some meat and enjoyed a meal of cold ham sandwiches and cool milk. Austin was silent throughout the meal and soon left for the fields again. He had a lot of thinking to do. He had spent the morning praying about God's will for his life. He realized that his own plans did not matter; God's plans were best. So he prayed that the Lord would reveal His will and he vowed to follow it.

Before he could make a final decision about Rebecca, he felt a need to go to his wife's grave. After the afternoon work, he walked up the little knoll to the place where he had buried his wife. She had often gone to this little knoll to pray. She said that looking over the prairie with its waving grass and ever-changing colors had given her peace. He would often come in early from the fields and play with the children so that she could go to her special place. It was the natural place to lay her to final rest.

He leaned down, pulled the weeds that were growing, and placed some field flowers he had picked on the way on the fresh soil. He knelt beside the small cross marker "Victoria, what should I do? Oh, I miss you so. If you were here, I would not have to make these difficult decisions. What should I do?"

Almost immediately, a conversation they had just before the twins were born came to mind. "Austin, if I don't make it through this, promise you'll find a mother for my children," she had said.

"Victoria, that's nonsense. You'll make it. I only want you to be the mother of our children."

"Austin, I could not bear the thought of my children growing up without a mama's arms to hug them and teach them. Promise me?"

Austin had hesitated, but the pleading look in his wife's eyes forced him to agree.

The recollection was so powerful, he threw himself on the grave and wept. He knew that Victoria's request long ago was God's plan now. He rose slowly from the ground and walked toward the house. He knew now what he must do; his own will could not enter into the decision. He decided that it was best to talk to Rebecca as quickly as possible. He imagined that she was worried about her future. After all, he had told her the day he met her that she could not stay. But, he wondered, will this plan bring her peace or more fear? Since it must be God's will, Austin decided that He would take care of Rebecca's emotions. It was Austin's job to obey and allow God to do the rest.

Austin entered the house and found Rebecca at the stove fixing supper. He smiled at her, grateful that she had already taken over the chore he least liked.

At his entrance, Rebecca tensed. She had sensed the somber mood that he displayed during the day and had become fearful that it was caused by something that she had done wrong. She was afraid that at some point, he would direct his frustration toward her. He had never given her a reason to think that way, but years of abuse were hard to forget.

Grateful that the food was ready, she placed a plate full of venison on the table. She had found some carrots and potatoes in the cold room and had boiled them together. She had also discovered the garden and wondered whose chore it would be. She had never worked in a garden, but hoped that she could learn. The thought of starting out with seeds, soil, and water and ending up with carrots and beans excited her. It was a place she could see new life, instead of the death and pain she had already experienced. She stopped herself from dreaming too much. She could not plan a future where there wasn't one. She looked at the meal she placed on the table and hoped it would at least be acceptable to him for now.

She sat down at the table with the little family and kept her eyes on her plate as Austin served each child and then her. Just as she was about to take a mouthful, she heard Austin's strong voice, "Thank Thee, Lord, for your provision. Bless the hands that made this food, and bless our family. Amen." She bowed her head to cover the blush that formed on her delicate, pale face. How could she forget that he began each meal the same way? She chided herself for the mistake.

Austin didn't seem to notice Rebecca's embarrassment, or her uneasiness about the meal and began to eat. When he seemed to be enjoying the food she prepared, Rebecca relaxed a little and began to eat as well. It was very good, she realized with slight surprise and a small swell of pride. At least she had done something well.

Austin listened to the girls chatter on about their day and glanced occasionally at Rebecca who seemed very occupied in the meal before her. The children were happy with the way she had taken care of them that day. He was relieved that they had adjusted to her care so quickly.

Rebecca felt nervous with Austin in the house and wished that he would finish eating and return to his work. But he seemed in no hurry to retreat from the room and continued to listen to the girl's stories.

Eventually, after the simple supper, he went to the barn to do his chores. With a strong desire to share his decision with Rebecca that evening, Austin hurried with the chores and returned to the house to find her attending to the baby and listening to the children. No, the children would not have trouble accepting the girl. He was convinced of that. He greeted the children and sent them off to bed. He sat down in a chair near Rebecca and looked at her.

Her innocent eyes did not at that moment betray her tortured past. Austin was afraid that what he had to say to her just might change their pallor. "Rebecca, can we talk?"

Rebecca looked up at him in fear. She was afraid that it was time for him to send her away. What would she do? How could she take care of herself and a baby? She tried not to show her fear and quickly masked the look in her eyes, but not before Austin saw its presence.

"Rebecca, I would really like for you to stay here and help with the children, and you need help with your baby, too. But, uh, you can't stay in our home. People would talk."

Rebecca kept her head down. She had learned long ago it was the quickest defense against her father's tirades, yet she did not receive one from Austin. Austin took a deep breath and plunged into the words he had rehearsed, "Mrs. White thinks that the best solution for both of us is to get married."

Rebecca gasped. Marriage? The memory of her last "marriage" loomed heavily in her mind. She felt the desire to bolt from the room and forced her quivering hands to be still. Austin saw the fear in her face and prayed silently for the Lord to help her make her decision. Was she, too, grieving her dead spouse? Was he asking too much of her? She had only been a widow for a short time. He sat quietly waiting for Rebecca to respond.

Rebecca knew that she truly had no choice. Marriage was not her picture of a perfect solution but, she had to provide for the life that was growing inside of her. She would have to forget about her own fears and needs to think about the baby. Austin seemed to be good with his own children. Would he treat her baby with kindness, too?

She said, hardly above a whisper, "I'll marry you."

Austin sighed. It was final. "We'll do it as soon as the traveling minister comes through, alright?"

She shook her head, yes, unable to control her emotions to speak.

"Goodnight, Rebecca," Austin said, walking from the room to give her some time to be alone. His heart ached for her, for her loss that he knew so well. He turned back and said softly, "Everything will be okay."

Rebecca heard what he said but did not take much consolation in his promise. Hadn't every man she'd known betrayed her?

Chapter 9

$\mathcal{A}$ustin lay down on his little make shift bed. "Well, I did it," he thought. There's no turning back now. He had half hoped that she would say no and half hoped for a yes. He did need help. He knew that he could lose all that he had without her help. He also realized how much the children needed a mother after seeing the change in them just the few days of her care. He had not realized, in his own grief, how the girls had been affected by their mother's absence. It had been a hard, but wise decision.

In the days that followed, Rebecca felt strong enough to take on more of the chores required to run the house and take care of the children, so she did it with a fervor. She was still concerned that Austin would find fault with her and send her away. Although she did not relish the thought of being married to him, she did not have a choice and feared being sent away even more than she feared marriage. Austin warned her to take care of herself, but she was fearful that he would change his mind if he thought she was lazy.

The third morning after the proposal, Rebecca rose and took time to study the house for the first time. There were cobwebs in the rafters, and the wooden floor was covered with mud and dirt. Even the children looked disheveled. She wondered where to begin first. No use cleaning up the children until the house was clean. She figured they would be filthy again quickly. So, with great resolve, she began dusting the kitchen. She lifted the rugs and hung them up on ropes she found out in the yard. She found a broom and began beating them. The girls ran giggling around her, but soon lost interest and sat on the porch to play with the baby. Rebecca hoped that they would keep the baby occupied long enough for her to get her work done. After beating the rugs, she swept the floor as best she could.

She stopped long enough to make a simple lunch for Austin and sent the twins with it to the fields. She didn't want him to return until she was finished.

Austin wondered why Rebecca had sent the meal up to him, but he was grateful that he did not have to stop very long from his labors. He quickly ate the food and drank the cool spring water before returning to his work.

When the girls returned, Rebecca fed them and put them down for naps. Then she preceded to take all the dishes off the shelves, wipe the shelf clean, and rewash the dishes. She discovered tins full of staples she had not known were there and planned future meals in her head as she worked.

Finally, she stepped back, and with a rarely seen smile, admired the fruit of her labors. The children began to stir. She changed the baby and realized that he didn't have any clean clothes. She checked the girls' supply and realized the same was true for them. She knew what she'd be doing the next day. She fed the baby and then began to prepare the evening meal. There was no sign of Austin, so Rebecca fed the children, sent them off to bed, and cleaned the dishes. She left a plate on the stove to keep warm, and exhausted, she went to bed, too.

When Austin returned from the fields, he was pleasantly surprised to walk into the immaculately clean kitchen. He found his warm meal and smiled. It was good to have a woman around again. He didn't realize how much he had missed a good meal and a clean home. He crawled into his make-shift bed that night with a prayer on his weary lips for his little family.

~*~

The next morning Rebecca noticed that they would soon be out of the bread Mrs. White had so graciously provided. Well, Rebecca determined, it was time for her to start that chore as well. But first the wash needed to be done. She scrubbed the clothes as best she could and hung them on the line to dry. Then, looking at the curtains and bed clothes, she decided they needed a washing as well. All the while, the children played in the yard and the baby lay contented in the little basket at Rebecca's side.

She again sent the girls with a lunch for Austin and continued her chores. After she fed the children their lunch and waited for the clothes to dry in the breeze, she worked with the bread dough. She laid some dough aside and called the girls inside to suggest that they make cinnamon rolls. She had found a small tin of cinnamon on the shelves the day before. The girls clapped with glee and soon were washed and standing on chairs around the table. Rebecca patiently showed them how to roll the dough with the rolling pin. They each took a turn. Rebecca spread the dough with butter and gave the girls sugar and the cinnamon to sprinkle on top. Then with six helping hands they carefully rolled the bulging concoction into a log shape. Rebecca sliced the dough and set each roll on a tray to rise. Rebecca smiled at the memory of the times that she had helped her mother bake. She marveled at how good it felt to teach the girls something her own mother had taught her. A tear came to her eye, and she quickly brushed it away. She had no time for loneliness for her mother, instead she had a new family to take care of.

She stood back and noticed that the girls were covered with flour and cinnamon. She smiled and decided today was the day for a bath. She had spotted a big tub earlier and carried it to the kitchen. She heated big kettles of water on the fire and poured them into the tub. She tested the water for the right temperature and helped each of the girls to take her turn in the water.

She scrubbed each girl's hair and then her skin until it was pink. The girls laughed and splashed in the water as they took their turns. She dressed them in clean clothes from the line. Rebecca longed to climb in when they were done. But what if Austin returned? She decided to have Kristie and Carrie stand guard and quickly stripped down and stepped into the tub. It felt good to have a bath and wash her hair. The warmth of the water seemed to loosen her tired muscles. She had not realized how much they ached. This work was no harder than that which she had done back at home, but she had been traveling and recovering for a long time. She did not linger though, and soon she was out of the tub, had it emptied and placed it back on its peg.

She looked at the children as she served them their supper later. They looked so sweet and clean. She gave each of them a hug and could smell the fresh air in their clothes. She smiled and felt good about the accomplishments of the day. For dessert she gave them a piece of cinnamon roll, and after they licked their fingers, and exclaimed how yummy the rolls were, she shooed them off to bed into fresh clean bed clothes.

She placed a plate again for Austin on the stove along with a cinnamon roll. Barely able to keep her eyes open, she fed the baby and retired.

~*~

Austin entered the house after staying in the fields until dark. The smell of baked bread and cinnamon made him smile. He found his supper ready for him and savored the potatoes with bits of ham, corn from last year's crop and the best cinnamon roll he had ever eaten. He smiled as he bit into it and wondered how Rebecca found the energy to do so much more than look after the children.

He was even more surprised when he crawled into his bed to smell and feel freshly washed bedding. It was the best night's sleep he had since long before Victoria had become bedridden and it wasn't just the clean sheets that provided the good rest.

~*~

The next day, Rebecca rose with a fervor to tackle the bedroom. Once again, Austin had already risen and was in the fields. She felt little pangs of guilt at the thought of him getting his own breakfast. She poured herself some coffee and noticed that two cinnamon rolls were missing from the remaining ones and smiled at the knowledge that she had at least provided his breakfast that day. After feeding the children their breakfast of porridge already prepared by their father and waiting on the stove, she dusted and swept out the bedroom. She started to clean out the drawers in the wardrobe, but realized that Victoria's clothes still remained. Feeling like an outsider for the first time that week, she closed the drawer and decided to work in the children's room instead.

She sent a lunch to Austin again, but this time tucked a cinnamon roll in with the other food. The girls went chattering to the field, and Austin stopped his plowing and led them to a tree for shade. A smile appeared on his face when he saw another cinnamon roll waiting for him on his plate. The girls exclaimed, "Papa, we helped make the cin'min rolls. Do you like them?"

Austin laughed, "They are the best things I ever tasted."

It was those words that the girls reported to Rebecca as they entered the house after returning from delivering the meal.

"He really said that?" Rebecca asked in surprise. The girls nodded and sat down to their own lunch. Rebecca smiled feeling pride in her accomplishment.

"Yes, and he said that we all looked really pretty and smelled so nice and clean," Carrie chirped.

"We told him about the big tub, and he said he wished he could get a bath, too!" chimed in Kristie.

~*~

So that night, it wasn't only a warm supper that greeted Austin as he entered his home, but the tub waiting for him and a pot on the stove full of hot water. He added the hot water in the tub and quickly took a bath. It felt good to get the grime of work off of his skin. Washing up at the pump each night wasn't always enough.

After dressing in clean clothes, he took his plate from the stove and found a delicious meal and a huge piece of cobbler. He contemplated tapping on the door to thank Rebecca, but he knew that it would probably just frighten her. So he retired with a grin on his face and slept soundly.

Growing up, Rebecca had never truly thought about beautiful weddings and gowns like other girls. She never even thought it possible to escape from her lot. But watching Erin's wedding, she realized what she had missed. She couldn't fathom one like her friend's, but did dream now of a ceremony all her own. A simple, but beautiful dress with crocheted lace at her throat and wrists, one friend to stand at her side, a simple bouquet of flowers, a true minister, and a man that would love her like Thomas appeared to love Erin; that was what she longed for, but with a loveless marriage of convenience that was ahead of her, she didn't expect any of it, except perhaps the minister.

Picturing her present wardrobe, she wished at least that she had a nice dress and maybe some wild flowers braided in her hair. She opened her satchel in an unwarranted hope of a miracle. She pulled out the two ragged dresses that had stains and mended tears. They were not any better than the one she was wearing. Next came the singed traveling dress that had at one time made her feel equal to those around her. Now the smoke smell caught her breath and made her stomach rumble in memory of the stress-filled trip. There was no salvaging that one. There was one more dress at the bottom. She pulled it out trying to picture which one it was. It was the one that was torn by her husband on that horrific night. She gasped as she held it in her hands. The smell of him filled her nostrils causing her stomach to churn and bring bile into her throat. She began hysterically to shred it until it was unrecognizable. She ran into the other room and threw it into the fire.

Now she wished that she had accepted the dress that Erin had offered her. At the time she thought that all she would need was a work dress until she had made enough money to buy material to make a new one. She guessed the one she had been wearing would have to do for a wedding ceremony no use worrying about finding something better. After all, she was simply entering another arranged marriage, so her dreams of a special wedding day to a faithful man would never be fulfilled. If she couldn't have a man who she loved why worry about the other ceremony details?

Much to her surprise, though, Mrs. White had a different idea in mind and came to visit with plans to make the wedding more than Rebecca would have ever imagined.

Rebecca had just fed the baby and put him down for his nap. She had fed the girls, and they were dozing on their beds as well when she heard the clatter of a wagon outside. She peered out the window and saw Mrs. White making her way to the door.

Rebecca glanced around the kitchen and surmised that it looked pretty good in spite of the lunch dishes still on the table. She swung open the door and practically threw herself into Mrs. White's arms. Mrs. White was pleasantly surprised to receive the warm reception.

She immediately noticed the work that Rebecca had done in the kitchen and with Rebecca beaming before her, exclaimed, "Rebecca, the kitchen looks so nice. You've been working hard!"

Rebecca led her to the table and quickly served her a cup of coffee and a piece of cobbler. After chit chat about the children and the house, Mrs. White asked, "How are your wedding plans?"

Rebecca looked at her in surprise, "How did you know I said yes?"

"When Austin sent word that he would be needing the services of the traveling minister, I assumed that was the case."

"Oh," Rebecca said looking down at her hands.

"I know it is so soon after your husband's death, but it is a hard life here in the west, and hard times call for hard decisions. Austin is a good man. He will take good care of you and the baby."

Rebecca's face showed remorse, and Mrs. White assumed it was due to her loss, "I understand what it is like to lose someone you love."

Rebecca did not look up at the older woman. She did not want to hide the truth about her first husband from Mrs. White, but she could not speak of such an awful thing. Telling Erin had been terribly hard, but she did it in hopes of sparing her pain. She couldn't bear telling her story again, so she looked up at Mrs. White questioningly.

"I, too, lost someone I loved. Would you like me to tell you about it?"

Rebecca nodded.

"I was engaged to be married. We had been childhood friends. He and I had spent many hours walking in the woods, fishing and playing together. As we grew up, we still enjoyed to be together. I realized one day that I wanted to spend the rest of my life with him. I told my Mama and she said that I was in love," Mrs. White chuckled, and her eyes shone with the memory. "Then she told me it was a rare gift and I should not let Robert get away. So, I was really surprised when Robert asked me to our first grown up dance. Y'know he asked me that night to marry him when we became older. But Robert did not grow up," she said sadly. "He died of pneumonia the following winter."

Rebecca gasped and gingerly reached out her hand to cover Mrs. White's.

"So, you see, I understand what it is like to grieve. But, in this provision, God gave me Mr. White and though I still miss Robert and think of him occasionally, I am happy now and I love my husband. The hurt you feel now will go away, and God will give you a love for Austin. I promise."

Rebecca felt remorse over keeping the truth from Mrs. White. She sighed and tried to find the words to tell her of her wedding night, but Mrs. White interrupted her by placing something on the table.

"Here, honey, I made a wedding dress for you."

Rebecca's eyes shone as she looked at the pale blue dress trimmed in simple lace and picked it up in her hands. She looked at the delicate pink flowers and smiled, "Mrs. White, it is so beautiful. But..."

"It's okay, honey, consider it a wedding gift. You got to look pretty for your wedding day! The preacher is going to be here this Sunday."

Rebecca gasped with surprise. She had not expected it to be so soon, but why put it off any longer? Mrs. White ignored the look on Rebecca's face and added, "Now, go hide it so it'll be a surprise for Austin."

Rebecca obeyed and hid the dress in her luggage. The women spent the rest of the afternoon talking and making plans for the wedding day. After Mrs. White left, Rebecca realized that she was actually a little excited about the ceremony. Mrs. White was going to make it extra special, and she had gotten the dress of her dreams.

She had come to trust the older woman. Mrs. White wouldn't suggest that she marry someone who would be wrong for her, would she?

~*~

Despite Mrs. White's reassurance and support, the wedding day came too soon for both Austin and Rebecca. They had not seen each other all week with Rebecca rising after he left for the fields and retiring before he returned, so Sunday morning was very tense as they both entered the kitchen. Rebecca had risen earlier than Austin this day and had prepared a delicious breakfast of slices of thick bacon, pancakes with jam, and hot coffee that tasted better than anything Austin had made the last few weeks.

Austin changed into a clean shirt and pants. He went out to the barn to check the stock and get the horse hitched to the wagon. He returned to find his little family standing in a line with clean brushed hair. The girls had theirs in braids and the view of his daughters made him smile. But the sight that truly caught his eye was Rebecca. She stood before him in a new calico dress with a shy look on her face as she seemed to be studying the floor.

Austin whistled and said, "You girls look beautiful. <u>All</u> of you," he said, making it a point that Rebecca knew he included her. She blushed and he smiled at her. He ushered the girls to the waiting wagon while Rebecca gathered up the baby and joined Austin at the wagon. He effortlessly lifted her up to the seat and climbed up beside her. His closeness unnerved Rebecca, but she held her ground and refused to move away from him. He would soon be her husband, and she would have to be even closer to him. The thought brought back memories of her first wedding night, and she shuddered. She turned her face away and fought back the tears that threatened to burst out.

Austin urged the horse on to the dusty road and traveled in silence. He, too, was in deep thought. He was doing something that went against every emotion that he had. He could only rely on what he knew to be God's will so he pressed his emotions down and repeated the words, "Thy will be done," over and over in his mind.

Rebecca, on the other hand, was having second thoughts. She considered telling Austin to let her off the wagon and call the wedding off, but she knew that she could not make that choice. She had to consider her unborn child. She placed her hand on her stomach and closed her eyes. She prayed to the God that she had trusted all through her traveling to the west. She had to trust Him now. In God's hands. In God's hands. The words gave her comfort, and she looked at Austin from the corner of her eye. He seemed harmless. He had been good to her. Would he change once he married her and she no longer had a choice or an escape like her mother? Surely, if her mother had known what kind of man her father was, she would not have married him. She wished now that she had insisted on her mother telling her about her early days of married life. She prayed or more so begged God to make her child's life better than her own.

Austin's thoughts turned to the day he married Victoria. He had loved her from the first time he saw her. Their wedding day was extra special, filled with laughter and teasing. He had never known something was as right as that day he had married her. He longed to reach out and hold her again. He shook his head as if trying to stop the flood of memories. He would soon have a new wife, and Victoria was gone. He must make the best of this new situation for Rebecca and the children. It was God's will. He must follow that will, or he would never be happy again. He clucked to the horses to pick up their step and leaned forward with a resolve to obey his God.

They continued to ride the two miles to the church in silence. If it were not for the chattering of the children, the silence would have driven Rebecca back to the safety of her bedroom.

Chapter 10

*I*t was a beautiful day, and neighbors from all around came to join in what they thought was Rebecca and Austin's joy. Neither groom nor bride revealed their true feelings to the well-wishing friends. No one noticed that behind the smiles and words of thanks was pain and turmoil.

The minister said the vows and asked Rebecca if she pledged to love, honor, and obey Austin until death do them part. She teetered as she became light-headed, but Austin's firm hold around her waist kept her from falling. She wondered about the love pledge. Was she lying to God by saying yes? She did not really know much about God and hoped that He would understand when she said "I do."

Austin spoke his vows as a prayer and pledge before God, hoping that the emotions would come as the two worked side by side together. He squeezed Rebecca's waist gently as he said, "I do."

She looked up at him and saw compassion written on his face. She cried out in her heart and could only hope that what she saw there was true.

"You may now kiss the bride," the minister announced.

Austin saw the look in Rebecca's eyes at those words and although it appeared so to the rest of the crowd, his lips did not touch hers. He pulled his head away, and Rebecca sighed and truly looked into his eyes for the very first time since she first met him. Their emerald green hue seemed to say to her, trust me. But how could she? There was more to fear later.

Austin put his arm around her, turned toward his friends, and smiled. The friends cheered and rushed to them with well wishes. Rebecca was overwhelmed by their excitement so much so that Austin had to lead her away.

The newlyweds walked toward the tables full of special treats for the occasion. It was only Austin's strong arms that made it   possible for Rebecca to walk steadily. Even the tantalizing plates of meat, vegetables, potatoes, and a table full of pies and cakes did not appeal to her. Her stomach churned at the thought of what she had just done. But she had to keep up appearances, so took the plate Austin offered her. The girls ran toward them and hugged them both.

Once they had sat down on a blanket under a tree, Austin leaned toward her and whispered in her ear, "Rebecca, it will be okay. I promise."

Mrs. White had been holding the baby and came over. Rebecca reached for the baby but Mrs. White announced, "We will keep the children for you tonight."

Rebecca looked up at her with fear and quickly ducked her head back down. She was married now. Of course she would need to be alone with her husband tonight. But all the reasoning could not stop her hands from quivering.

After what seemed to be hours of introductions and well wishes, Austin led Rebecca to the wagon and helped her up. He swung up beside her and waved at the children and the neighbors as he whistled for the horses to go.

Rebecca shivered, and Austin put his arm around her. He felt her tense at his touch and quickly removed his arm. They rode on in silence, but Rebecca did not notice for the raging thoughts that kept racing through her mind. It seemed that the night before her flight from Ireland replayed itself over and over. She had vowed that next day never to go through what had happened to her at the hands of her husband again. She had hoped that America held the key to the release from her torture, but instead it had led her right back into a marriage again. Soon, she would suffer at another man's hands. What if the baby was hurt? What had she allowed to happen?

She was surprised when the wagon came to a stop. They had pulled up to the house. She began to shiver.

Austin went around to help her down, and again she cringed at his touch. He saw the terror in her eyes and gasped. Did he cause that terror? Her palpable fear was much stronger than he imagined. He had thought that she had been hesitant about the wedding because of her love for her first husband, but what he saw in her eyes was far more than that. She was afraid of him! What could cause such fear in one so young? Austin remembered her cries of fear when she first came. He had assumed they were from fear of her father, for she cried his name out many times. He released her and mumbled, "I'll put the horses to bed," and turned, leaving her standing in the yard as he led the horses to the barn. Rebecca stared after him for a while, not able to move her numb body. Eventually, the cool evening air stirred her on, and she entered the house and lit the lamps.

Austin hesitated in the barn struggling with his own emotions. He knelt down in the hay to talk with the Lord.

"Lord, you know that I love Victoria. You also know all that Rebecca has gone through in her young life. She's afraid of me. Someone has hurt her deeply and Lord, she's just a child."

After quite a long while, he rose with the knowledge that the Lord confirmed that this marriage would be in name only for now.

Rebecca heard Austin enter the house and tried to still the fear that rose up in her throat as if to gag her. She listened to every sound he made in fear of the inevitable. She had changed into the nightgown Mrs. White had given her and had already crawled into bed to wait for her new husband.

Austin blew out the lamps and crawled into the make shift bed that he had slept in during the few weeks since Rebecca came. He had a resolve that it was best for Rebecca for them to be apart tonight. He hoped that his action sent her a message that he could be trusted.

Rebecca's heart-beat returned to normal as the time wore on she realized that Austin was not joining her. She closed her eyes and tried to sleep. Eventually she did dose off, but the stress of the day and the fears of the past came to haunt her through a terrible nightmare.

~*~

Austin awoke, hearing her screams and was unsure of what to do. Would his presence make her scream more? He prayed for wisdom. When she continued to scream, he rose from the bed, lit a lamp, and went to her room. "Rebecca," he said softly. He said it louder and louder until she stopped screaming and opened her eyes. He could see the panic and fear there, but he knew this time it was not from his presence but from the past.

He set the lamp down and walked slowly toward her. Remembering how reading the Scriptures had calmed her in the past, he began quoting from memory one of the Psalms.

He sat down at the edge of her bed. At the sound of his strong, peaceful voice, Rebecca wept.

Austin put his arm around her, and when she did not pull away, he pulled her close, all along speaking God's Word to her. For the first time in her life, Rebecca felt safe. She clung to Austin and continued to weep. He whispered to her and held her for a long time.

He said, "Rebecca, you're safe here. I won't do anything to hurt you, and I won't let anyone else hurt you."

Rebecca wanted to believe him, but years of abuse were hard to forget. For now she allowed herself to hope that he was telling the truth.

Austin did not know how long he sat whispering words of encouragement to Rebecca. After she had long fallen asleep in exhaustion, he sat with her in his arms and prayed for her. As he held her, he sensed that the Lord was knitting his heart with hers. He knew that if it was necessary he could hold her and encourage her for the rest of their lives. A verse from Ephesians came to his mind, "Husbands love your wives, even as Christ also loved the church, and gave Himself for it." In that instant, he knew that there was a love in his heart for her. He had given himself up for her, in a sense, when he chose to marry her. He sensed the love that a husband would have for a wife begin to spring up in his heart. That love that he had read about so often in the Bible became clear to him. It was a command and he realized, that as he had obeyed God and had pledged himself to this woman, God had honored the commitment and had given him the love that he needed to be her husband. He knew that it was not the same kind of love that he had for Victoria, but it was a new love that he could display to his new wife and use to build a life together with her.

~*~

Rebecca awoke to find Austin sitting on the floor beside her bed sleeping, leaning against the bed frame, with one hand on her arm. She realized that his touch did not make her cringe. The memory of the nightmare and his gentle voice reminded her of why she felt differently than before. He had promised that she could trust him, and he kept his word. Her second wedding night had proven not to be like the first. She slipped out of the bed without rousing him and went to the kitchen to make them breakfast. He joined her at the smell of coffee and sat down at the table.

She turned to him and smiled at his tousled hair and sleepy face and poured him a cup. They did not talk, but it was not a strained silence like the previous day.

They dressed, and Austin hitched the horses to go and retrieve the children. As Austin lifted Rebecca up onto the wagon seat, he looked at her tattered dress and said, "Is that all you have to wear?"

Rebecca did not look at him but peered down at her dress. "I have my traveling dress, but it's not in much better shape, and, she hesitated, a little embarrassed, "my wedding dress."

Austin chastised himself for not noticing Rebecca's need.

"We will need to go to town and buy you what you need. Your shoes do not look much better than your dress. You will need warm boots for the winter. The children probably need things, as well and we have a new baby coming. You'll want some things for him."

"I can use the clothes Ryan has grown out of."

"You'll still want some new things. I remember how excited Victoria would be about making new outfits for each of the children. Of course, she was caught off guard when the twins came, but she had made so many things that she had plenty.

Rebecca nodded her head in agreement, as Austin swung up beside her and clucked at the horse.

Rebecca was surprised at how much she had missed the children. At their arrival, the girls ran to both her and Austin and hugged them. Rebecca's heart leapt as the children told her they had missed her, too. Their hugs brought tears to her eyes. She took the baby from Mrs. White's arms and held him close. He grinned when he saw her and reached out his arms to her. Austin smiled at her and put his arm around her as she held his son. She looked up at him, and he could see in her eyes a true sense of belonging.

Austin helped his little family into the wagon, thanked the Whites, and steered the horses toward home with a grin on his face that could be read by all as pride.

They returned to their home, and Rebecca knew that the girls were happy to be back. Austin decided to go to the fields with a promise of a trip into town the next day.

"If we are going to town tomorrow, I need to work in the fields today."

Rebecca was relieved at the thought of him not being in the house.

On his way out the door, he told Rebecca to check their supplies and make a list of what they needed.

~*~

That night, after the children were tucked into bed. Austin came to her as she lay in the dark and in a voice barely above a whisper, he asked, "Rebecca, I can't continue sleeping on the floor. May I join you?"

He was asking permission to sleep in his own bed with his own wife! Rebecca wondered what made him so different than the other men in her life. She nodded her consent, and Austin crawled in beside her. She tensed at his nearness, but tried not to show it.

"Good night, Rebecca," Austin said as he turned his back toward her and covered up.

Rebecca soon heard his steady breathing of sleep and sighed with relief. She turned her back toward him and fell asleep without a repeat of the nightmare of the night before.

The next morning, Austin loaded the family into the wagon and rode toward town. Rebecca had been hesitant that morning as to what to wear. She came out in her mended dress. Austin took one look at her and told her to wear her wedding dress.

"You looked beautiful in it, and I want everyone to see how beautiful my wife is."

Rebecca blushed. She never thought of herself as beautiful; in fact her father had called her ugly. He said that she was so ugly that he would have to pay some man to marry her. Well, it ended up that someone had paid her father for her, she thought, remembering the money changing hands that night.

Rebecca had not seen the town since she arrived. The church was on the outskirts on a piece of land donated by an older couple, and the Finnigans did not pass through the town to get there.

She remembered little of her first visit. The last few days of her trip by train were a blur, and she only vaguely remembered getting a ride with the mercantile owner's son. She remembered little else.

To be fair, there was little in the town to remember in the first place. She spotted the mercantile with its neatly painted front and railed porch. She saw next to it a small house with a sign that simply said "Seamstress." There were several other buildings sporting signs that advertised a livery, a bank, a blacksmith, and a boarding house. There were a few small houses that did not look as large or as comfortable as Rebecca's new home.

The little family first climbed the wooden steps of the mercantile. Upon entering the shop, a flood of memories came back to her. She stood in the doorway as if frozen in time. Austin whispered in her ear, "Rebecca, are you okay?"

"Becca, aren't you going in?" asked Kelly Anne as she tugged on Rebecca's dress.

Rebecca backed out of the door and stood on the walk, trying to catch her breath. Austin joined her and put his arm around her. She buried her head in the soft cotton of his shirt. He looked up, hoping not to create a scene, and led her to the side.

"Rebecca, what's the matter?"

"My father owns a shop just like this one. I have worked in it ever since I could remember."

Austin tilted Rebecca's head up so that he could look into her eyes. He saw a tear there, and with his thumb he wiped it off. Surprising, but not unwelcome, he fought the urge to kiss it away. "We're not in your father's shop. He is far away from you and can never harm you again. You're with me and I will never let anything bad happen to you. Come on, take my hand, and we'll go back in together." He put out his hand and gestured for her to take it.

Rebecca placed her small hand into her husband's large callused hand. It felt good there, and she looked up at Austin with a smile. He smiled back, and a sense of calm came over her. They walked into the building again. Austin gave their list of food items to the owner, Mr. Conley. He recognized Rebecca and told her how glad he was to see her in better health.

Rebecca smiled at him and answered, "Thank you, thank you so much for your help that day."

"We look after each other in this town. We have to; we never know when we'll need some help ourselves."

Austin led Rebecca to the area with the yard goods and stood by her side as together they chose material for clothes for the girls and the babies.

Austin picked up a calico, one of the most expensive pieces the store had to offer and showed it to Rebecca, "This would make a beautiful dress for you."

Rebecca reached out and caressed its softness, "Oh, Austin, it's beautiful, but it's too expensive."

"You deserve it, and besides we have had a good season. I can afford it." He picked out a dark gray wool and said, "You need to make a warm dress for the winter and also a cape or a coat. Do you know how to sew something like that?"

Rebecca shook her head, no, embarrassed by her lack of skill. Her mother had little time free to work on their clothes and had only taught her the necessary stitches, Besides, Rebecca did not consider herself very smart and doubted that she could learn to do such a thing.

"Well, we'll ask Mrs. Morgan. She's a seamstress. She can make you something really nice." He responded without judgment. He carried the bolts to the clerk for measurement.

"Now, let's find warm boots for the family. Kelly Anne can wear a pair of the twin's boots from last year, and the babies won't need any yet. We'll be carrying them," he said with a grin, remembering how it was to take care of two babies at once when the twins were born.

Rebecca and the twins tried on boots until they each found a pair that fit and met with Austin's strict requirements. Austin went to the counter and paid for all of the items he had chosen. When the girls weren't looking he even bought some candy for a surprise later. He winked at Rebecca and handed her the bag to hide the treats from the girls. She tucked them inside the baby's blankets and kissed the child's sleeping face.

~*~

Before they left town, Austin stopped at the seamstress shop. He decided to give her both of the bolts for Rebecca's things. "You don't have time to be sewing much more than the children's things," he said when she protested.

The seamstress, Mrs. Morgan smiled at Rebecca and said, "You have a good husband, Mrs. Finnigan."

Rebecca nodded and looked at Austin admiringly.

"I will need to get your measurements before you go. Mr. Finnigan, you can wait out in the parlor."

Austin stayed in the parlor as Mrs. Morgan led Rebecca into the sewing room. She directed Rebecca as to where to stand and quickly began measuring her. Noticing the size of her stomach, Mrs. Morgan said, "We will make the waist so that it will be able to grow with the baby, and when the baby has come, we can take it in. Come in next week and they'll be finished. Then you can try them on and see what you think."

Rebecca nodded appreciatively and returned to her husband in the parlor. Rebecca and the girls waved good-bye to Mrs. Morgan and returned to the wagon. Austin helped each one settle in, and they rode back to the farm contented with their purchases.

Chapter 11

The family continued the rest of their week with the same routine of the week before. Rebecca had little time to think about her new husband. She was too busy trying to make the family a comfortable home, keep up with the wash, and feed and care for the children. She spent the evening hours tackling the clothes she had to make.

She was grateful for all the years of training at home. From a very young age, her father had insisted that she learn to run the house. He wanted his wife in the shop as much as possible, and her mother was constantly trying to appease her husband by waiting on him from morning until night.

Austin continued to spend hours in the fields. The months taking care of his first wife, then the baby, then Rebecca had left the fields in disarray, but with hard work and long hours he was starting to see an improvement.

When there was no more light to work in the fields, Austin spent the evenings in the barn, for it too had work to be done. He cleaned out the stalls, fixed harnesses and tools

and when he could not work any longer he washed up and
dragged himself inside to collapse on the bed beside his new
wife.

~*~

By the end of the week Rebecca had developed a routine
of taking care of everyday things. She had been able to keep up
with the house back in Ireland, but now she had four children
to take care of as well. She realized that the chores she had
accomplished the first week could not be tackled on a routine
basis, because while she had concentrated on larger projects,
she had neglected the everyday tasks. However, she was glad
that she had taken the time to take care of the cleaning and
putting the house back into order. Even though she had
developed a good routine, Rebecca had exhausted herself.

Each day seemed to be the same. She would rise to find
Austin already gone to the fields, the coffee pot with fresh
coffee waiting for her on the stove, and a pot full of porridge
for her and the children. She felt pangs of guilt that she could
not get up and do her duty of making breakfast for her
husband, but she was silently grateful that it was one thing less
that she had to do. She would serve the girls and herself
breakfast and feed the baby. Then after breakfast, she had
dishes to wash, beds to make, goods to make and bake, and
laundry to wash. The laundry was overwhelming. The baby's
needs were great in itself. She seemed to wash clothes

continually. She hung them out in the warm air and would return to the house to fix the next meal. Often, just the laundry and the meals were all that she could find time to do.

Ryan was good for her, and for that she was grateful. When not doing chores or taking care of him, she was mediating between the girls' little squabbles or fixing a cut, or soothing tears. Sometimes she felt like crying along with them.

At the end of the day, with the children tucked into bed, she would collapse into her own bed as well. Most nights, she did not even hear Austin come in from the fields and crawl in beside her.

On Sunday morning, Rebecca rose and to her surprise, she found Austin still in the kitchen reading at the table. He looked up at her and smiled.

"Are you okay?" she asked, truly concerned.

"Yes, it's the Sabbath, the day of rest!"

"Oh," Rebecca replied remembering their wedding on the last Sabbath. She hurried over to the stove and found it already stoked. Austin had done it already, as he had every morning. She chided herself at her inability to rise before him and take care of the fire, the coffee, and his breakfast. This morning, though, he had only taken care of the fire and the coffee.

She was not used to Austin being around when she worked, and his presence made her feel nervous. Would he yell at her if her tasks were not completed correctly? She decided on the simplest meal and put water on to boil for porridge. She took the grain and tried to measure it out to pour into the boiling water. Her hand was shaking so hard that she spilt some on the floor. She gasped and looked over at Austin to see if he noticed. She felt the desire to flee to her room so as not to suffer his wrath but stood still, knowing that wherever she went, he would find her. Frozen, she stood with her eyes closed waiting for her punishment, but it did not come. Austin continued reading and did not look up.

She finished the coffee and placed it on the stove. She turned to take the bread from its cover and carefully sliced it into thick chunks. She heard the baby crying and turned suddenly, dropping half of the bread to the floor. This Austin did notice; he looked up to see her wide eyes of fear.

She fell to her knees with the memory of the jar she broke at the shop. She began picking up the pieces with shaking hands. "I'm sorry," she cried, "I'll clean it up."

"What was she afraid of, now?" Austin wondered. He knelt down, picked up the bread, and tossed it into the pig's slop pail. Rebecca closed her eyes and waited for his boot, but it never came.

"I'll get the baby," he said as he walked from the room, and Rebecca put her face in her hands and wept. In her heart she knew that Austin was a good man, but when certain situations arose she could not think rationally, she only remembered the past pains.

She stopped short when she heard giggling from the children's room and knew that the whole clan was awake. She enjoyed hearing the children play with their father and wished that her own father had played with her. Rebecca got up from the floor, wiped her tears, brushed off her dress and proceeded to finish preparing the meal.

Austin came into the kitchen holding the baby in one arm, Kelly Anne in the other, and the twins were clinging to his legs and laughing. Rebecca turned and smiled at the scene. Austin caught her grin and smiled at her, "What a bunch we've got here."

He paused, then said, "Girls, help your mama with the meal."

Rebecca was shocked at the name he had called her. He really did mean for her to be the children's mama. How would the girls react to the new name? They seemed not to notice, and stood before her for their instructions. She smiled and gave them each a hug, and with the honor of her new Mama role she gave the girls simple commands. "Kristie, you get the milk and the preserves from the cold room. Kelly Anne, you help Carrie to set the table."

The baby started to cry, and she turned to take him from Austin. He shook his head and smiled, "I don't get to feed him much anymore, and I miss it. I can do it."

Kristie retrieved the milk and preserves and helped Rebecca serve the porridge. Austin sat murmuring silly words to the baby, and Rebecca looked on in admiration of the father and his devotion to his children.

Once the meal was fixed and the children were all in their places, Austin told them all to bow their heads. He prayed a simple prayer to a God that Rebecca did not know but was beginning to desire to know: "Dear Lord, we thank thee for this meal. We thank thee for this family and for healthy children. We thank thee for this new mama that you have sent to us. Amen."

The children chimed in, "Amen."

Austin pretended not to notice the tear in Rebecca's eye. The prayer was so beautiful and she felt such acceptance that it brought tears to her eyes. He handed her a bowl of porridge, and she looked at him quizzically.

He met her look and asked, "What's wrong?"

"I ruined the bread," she replied assuming that she would not be eating breakfast because of her mistake.

"You still have more, and there's plenty of porridge."

Austin had no idea what thoughts were running through Rebecca's mind, but she began to eat the porridge with another tear in her eye. She had rarely experienced such kindness.

Carrie asked Rebecca, "What did you do on the Sabbath at your house?"

Rebecca gulped, "We...uh...we closed the shop on Sundays."

"Papa says we should only do what we have to do on the Sabbath. I like it. It's the best day of the week. We get to play with Papa and he doesn't go into the fields. Papa says that someday we'll have a   preacher every Sunday to go hear, and that we need to pray for God to send one."

"Until then," Austin explained, "we meet at the church and take turns with hymns and sharing from the Bible. We haven't been able to go since...for a while. Would you all like to go today?"

The children cheered, and Rebecca looked blankly at her husband. Having never been to church she did not know what to expect, but she nodded her head, yes. She knew that she could not refuse to go and she was also curious about what happened there. The people she had met on her wedding day seemed nice enough, and it would be good to see Mrs. White again.

"We need to leave as soon as everyone is ready. Girls, can you get your best clothes on? Carrie help Kelly Anne."

"I'm big enough to dress myself," Kelly Anne announced as she stood in front of her father.

"Well, that you are," the big man said as he lifted the little girl into his arms. He hugged her and kissed her neck, and she started to giggle. "Papa that tickles!"

He laughed and carried her to her room and dropped her to the bed. "This doesn't tickle, does it?" he said, as he tickled under her arms and her tummy. Kelly Anne was wiggling and laughing. The two other girls ran in and jumped on their father's back as if to rescue their little sister. Austin spun the two around and plopped them onto the bed beside their sister. Then he preceded to tickle all three of them.

Rebecca stood in the door way, hugging the baby to her chest, smiling at the scene before her.

"Mama; save us," cried Kelly Anne. Rebecca glowed with the little girl's name for her.

"I don't think I can. Your Papa is too big for me!"

"Your mama is a wise woman," he said standing erect and turning toward her with a smile. She smiled back, and for an instant Austin knew in his heart that his little family would be okay.

Every time Austin smiled at Rebecca it made her feel all warm inside. She was surprised how one smile could change a man's countenance. Laughter and silliness were not part of her growing up years, but now she realized it was another thing that she wanted her own child to experience. She thought of the baby inside her womb. He would be raised in this home of laughter and giggling. Would Austin treat him the same way he treats his own children?

"Come now, let's get ready for church," said Austin interrupting Rebecca's thoughts.

Rebecca hesitated at the doorway. She did not have much to wear. Should she wear the dress she wore on her wedding day? There was no other choice. She reluctantly dressed and re-entered the kitchen to meet Austin's gaze.

He smiled at her approvingly and Rebecca blushed.

"We need to get back to town this week so you'll have something else to wear. Do you want to go tomorrow?"

Rebecca nodded and made her way to the children's room.

With much direction from father and mother, the girls were all dressed with their hair combed and braided. They hurried out to the wagon. Austin helped Rebecca and the baby up onto the seat, and then he climbed up beside her.

~*~

This ride to the church was so much more pleasant than the last one. They rode along, listening to the girl's chatter as they pointed out wildlife and colorful flowers. Rebecca took a more observant look around her. The blue sky was spotted with white puffy clouds. The tall grass waved at her in the wind. She noticed that the colors changed as the wind blew the grass. She watched the shadows and light of the clouds and the rising sun displayed on the grass. It seemed that the green went on forever until it met the blue sky of the horizon.

As she concentrated on the scene before her, she noticed birds flying and wished that she could hear their singing above the sounds of the wagon and clip-clop of the horses. In front of them a gopher poked his head out of his hole and just as quickly ducked back down. Austin pointed it out to the children but before they had their gaze upon it, the gopher was gone.

Along the way, the Finnigans began meeting other families in their wagons. They each called their hellos as they waited their turn to enter the main road. Rebecca smiled as each family called her by name. They knew who she was already. Would she ever learn all of their names?

Soon they were in front of the church. Mrs. White spotted the little family, and with eyes gleaming, she came over and hugged Rebecca. "How are you, honey?"

Rebecca gave her best smile and said, "Fine." She was fine, just exhausted. She would get used to the feeling.

Rebecca smiled and proudly joined her husband as they entered the little church. Austin led them to a bench. Rebecca sat down and straightened her back. She felt pride in her little family, sitting quietly beside her. When had they become her family? Maybe it was when they called her mama or when she had wiped their tears after they scraped their knees. She couldn't pinpoint an exact moment, but she just knew that she felt warm inside at the thought of them.

The room was simple. There was a wooden cross at the front, a small table, and a handmade podium. Rows of benches lined the entire room, and almost every seat was taken. Rebecca and Austin sat in the middle which gave Rebecca the opportunity to look at some of the neighbors without turning around.

The group sang several songs that were unfamiliar to Rebecca, but she enjoyed them and listened closely to try to learn them. She had only been in a church once before, on the day she had married Austin.

Her only knowledge of God had come from that one kind woman who had tried to befriend her mother. But Rebecca's father was always there so her mother dared not talk to the woman for long. Rebecca admitted to absorbing all she had ever heard the woman say about God, but it was all confusing to her.

Rebecca realized with hope that her mother did have someone to turn to if she needed. She remembered the letter she sent her mother when the two ships had met. The woman would have received the letter by now. Rebecca hoped that she would return with the letter and continue to be a friend to her mother. She hoped the woman would show her mother kindness like she had experienced from Austin.

Someone stood up and read from a book like Austin had been reading from that morning. Rebecca listened and recognized some of the words from the times that Austin had read to her. She looked at him, and his eyes met hers. He smiled at her, and she blushed and looked down at little Ryan sleeping in her arms.

The service was soon over, and the congregation spilled out into the warm sunny day. Austin led his family to the wagon and helped them up. Other families were milling around laying out blankets and picnic lunches. Rebecca recognized some of them and nodded to Mrs. Morgan who was standing off with another family. Rebecca watched the families questioningly and looked at Austin. "Next week, we can bring a picnic lunch if you'd like and join 'em," he said.

Returning home, Rebecca swept into the kitchen to find something to fix for lunch. Austin followed her in, and noticing her slight panic over the chore said, "Rebecca, let's just have something simple. It's to be your day of rest, too."

She smiled at him gratefully and sent Carrie for some ham to be sliced and served cold. She placed slices of bread on the table and opened canned fruit.

After the meal was over Austin announced, "Let's give Rebecca a tour of the farm after lunch is cleaned up!"

Ready to agree to anything, the girls cheered and ran to the door.

Austin called them back, "Girls, first we need to clean up! Don't you help Mama with the chores when I'm in the fields?"

Rebecca heard the sternness in his voice and froze. Well, it had to happen eventually. No man could go that long without getting angry. She wanted to run into the bedroom and hide from him, but her love for the children overtook her fear, and she stayed.

"Rebecca, have you been doing all the chores yourself?"

She did not answer; she could not form the words to explain her determination to work for her keep. She couldn't tell him that she was afraid he would send her away if she did not do her job. Was he unhappy with her work? What did he want from the girls?

"Girls, come here," Austin said firmly. Rebecca closed her eyes, not wanting to see what Austin would do to them. Flashes of being beaten as a child came to her mind, and she felt dizzy.

Austin pulled the girls to him and reached out to Carrie caressing her face. He smiled at her and said, "Will you please help your mama with the chores?"

"Yes, Papa," she said with a smile.

"How about you, Kristie?"

"Sure, Papa," Kristie replied.

Kelly Anne chirped, "Me, too, Papa, I want to help Mama."

Austin hugged each child and explained to them what their chores would be for each meal. He glanced up at Rebecca and was surprised to see the look on her face. He rose from the chair and walked over to her, "Rebecca, what's wrong?"

She faltered before him, and he reached out to steady her. He told the girls to look after their brother and led Rebecca out into the sunlight.

He turned her to himself and said again, "Rebecca, what's wrong?"

How could she explain to him the fear that gripped her at a moment's notice, at his voice, his touch, his presence?

Feeling her cringe at his touch, he said, "Rebecca, I'm not your father. I will not strike you or the children, ever."

"How did you know about him?" she said, hurt showing in her eyes.

"You talked a lot when you were sick. I know what happened to you at the hand of your father."

She closed her eyes and wavered again. Austin dared to pull her to himself, and she did not resist. "Oh, Rebecca, I wish I could make those memories go away." He said, his lips so close to her ear she could feel his breath. "I wish I could have rescued you before he hurt you. But I couldn't. I can't make the hurt go away. The Lord can heal you of your pain."

Rebecca wept as she clung to him. This man was different. This man cared about her. She rested in his strong arms around her. With him she felt safe. Austin prayed for her, "Lord, you know the hurt in Rebecca's heart. Show her how much You love her and care for her. Heal her of the hurts. Help her to feel like she's a part of this family."

Austin held her for a few minutes and prayed silently that the love that he felt for her would flow through her and show her she had nothing to fear from him. He sensed though that it was nothing of his own doing that caused the times of fear; it was the past and its memories. Only time and the Lord would be able to erase those fears and heal Rebecca. Austin also sensed more than ever that there was more than just the fear of her father that haunted his new wife. What had her first husband done to her to put such fear of marriage in her?

He rocked Rebecca away slightly and wiped her tears from her face. He smiled at her, "Come on now, let's have some fun with our beautiful family, and listen, you need to get the girls to help you with the chores. You can't do it all yourself."

Rebecca looked at him with concern on her face.

"I mean it, Rebecca. You need to take care of yourself. You're going to have a baby, and we don't want anything to happen."

Chapter 12

They returned to the small kitchen to find that the girls had followed his instructions and were ready to go for their "tour."

They ran chattering around the couple as Austin picked up the baby and strode back outside.

The tour lasted all of the afternoon, though there was little to see. But each stop meant a new place for the children to explore, and they could always find a game to play. Their first stop was the well.

"Most farmers use a 'water witch' to find water," he told Rebecca. She looked at him quizzically.

"It's a y-shaped willow switch. They say when the switch trembles, it means there's water below, but I didn't use one. Instead I prayed, then I chose a spot to start digging and found water!"

The girl's favorite place was the barn. Austin piled up hay and the girls jumped from the ladder leading to the loft into it, giggling and crying for more. Rebecca sat down in a pile of clean hay with the baby in her arms and watched the girls and Austin play together. How she envied them. They loved and trusted him entirely. When he told them to jump into his arms they did so without hesitation. She bitterly asked the God she hardly knew why she did not have a father like Austin. What had she or her mother done to deserve such a wretched man?

She did not know, but assumed it must have been her fault somehow. She wondered if she would make God turn Austin into the same kind of man as her father. She shuddered at the thought. If Austin did change because of her, she would just leave. She still had the money she took from her first husband. Surely it would be enough to take her away. But where would she go? She hoped that she would not have to make that decision. She tried to push the thoughts from her mind.

After frolicking in the barn and talking to the cow the girls had named Milkie they continued their tour.

Their next stop was the chicken coop. The girls soon had the hens in a panic, and the rooster was strutting around trying to show them who was boss. The girls laughed as they chased the hens. Austin stood beside Rebecca and said, "Victoria demanded that we had chickens as soon as possible. So, I bought her a few." He fed them and gathered their eggs as he talked. "But when it came to butchering and plucking them, she demanded that I'd do it." He chuckled as he remembered it.

Rebecca saw the faraway look in his eye. "He still loves her," she thought. But of course; did she expect anything else? She was only here to help him with the children. She was a wife in name only. Why would she want anything else? She liked the convenience of living there without the "wifely duties" that she had learned quickly in her first marriage only meant pain and sorrow.

Austin was still talking, when Rebecca realized that she had not been listening. She looked at him and concentrated on his words. She heard him say something about getting one of the chickens and butchering it for her.

They continued their walk and passed a small building. It was made of grass. "This is a soddie," Austin explained. "It's what we lived in before we built the log house. I worked for the railroad for a few years and made enough money to buy this land, build Victoria a real home, and buy the seed I needed. Now I use the soddie to store things." He continued, "To build the soddie we cut big layers of sod from the ground and stacked them up like huge bricks to make the house. Hardly a day went by that Victoria didn't find a critter of some kind scampering at her feet or hanging from the ceiling. She was mighty glad when we moved out of there."

Rebecca peered inside of the little building and winced at the thought of living there. Still, Victoria had done it for the man she loved. Rebecca asked herself, if she would be willing to sacrifice for him as well.

After leaving the soddie, the family walked toward a row of   cottonwoods. The trees waved in the wind. "Did the wind ever stop blowing?" Rebecca wondered. In the midst of the trees was a small stream. They startled a deer that was drinking. It joined another deer that was lying in the shadow of a tree. Together they walked off to find a quieter place. The girls started running after them, but they were gone in an instant.

"You'll never get close to them that way, girls," laughed Austin.

Rebecca watched the graceful animals run off. She had never seen a wild animal so close, and it thrilled her. The deer were not the only wildlife to be found. As Rebecca sat down on the bank and became aware of her surroundings she spotted white-tailed rabbits hopping across the grass and she heard a squirrel chattering at her from a branch above as if scolding her for disturbing his quiet place. She saw several kinds of birds. She wished she knew their names, but she didn't ask.

"Watch out for snakes," Austin warned. At that announcement, Rebecca pulled her legs up underneath her dress, and Austin grinned at her. She blushed, but kept her legs where they were.

The water looked appealing and seemed to beckon the children. The girls begged Austin to go in, and he agreed. When it came to anything requested by those girls, it was hard for him to say no, Rebecca realized. Austin and the girls took off their shoes and socks, and Austin rolled up his pant legs. They begged Rebecca to join them, but she sat on the bank and shook her head.

Austin asked her one more time and then walked to the side of the creek to point out to the girls the wildlife living there. Rebecca leaned forward interested in what he had to say.

"Look girls, a frog," he said pointing to an area not far from them.

Rebecca could not contain her curiosity and stood to join Austin as he pointed out long-legged water bugs gliding across an area of still water. Rebecca's intrigue overcame her shyness, and she asked him to show her the frog she missed. Noting Rebecca's interest, Austin pointed out the minnows swimming together in the shallow places. Then he turned and led the girls into the water. The girls began splashing their father immediately.

Rebecca carried the baby to a grassy spot and sat down. She longed to join her new family, but a resistance that she had never experienced rose inside of her. At her father's hand she had no room for anger, joy, and contentment, only degrading fear and submission. She had to feel and be what he wanted. But in Austin's home, she could be stubborn if she wanted. With a new realization, it occurred to her that Austin would allow her to be who she was. The question was: who was she?

Emotions that had been pushed deep inside of her seemed to be coming to the surface. She realized that her defiance was not directed toward Austin but her father. The grief she felt as she lay in Austin's bed those days after her arrival had been new to her. She had known that she was unhappy back at her home, but did not realize the grief that the years of abuse had given her. Her only true emotion was out of survival. She had ignored the emotions because she knew she would suffer the consequences if she displayed them.

She realized now that she had never had the opportunity to be a real child. She wanted to run free like the children did in the water and cast off the burden of being a wife and mother. After all, she was only a child herself. What kept her from that freedom? What kept her from enjoying this time with her new family? Her lack of participation wasn't hurting Austin and the girls. She was the only one suffering from it. But still she sat on the side watching them as if she was glued to the spot. Maybe time would help her pain. Maybe one day she'd feel free enough to play beside them.

Soon the children were scrambling up beside her and putting their socks and shoes on again. Rebecca stood and followed them for the rest of the tour. They walked along the fields, and Austin pointed out the rows of corn, wheat, hay, oats, and a section of cabbage, squash, and potatoes. "The Lord's been good to us this year. No bugs, no drought, no fires. I pray every day for a good day, and He provides. It wasn't always so, and it might not always be again. We need to be good stewards of what He has provided this year. We might not have it so good in the future."

Rebecca wondered what made a man stay in a place so unpredictable. She wished she could ask him, but dared not to. They continued on, and the children ran ahead. Austin called them back, but they did not stop until they reached the top of a small knoll. Austin frowned and followed them. Rebecca walked behind him and gasped as she realized that the children were standing at a grave. Was it Victoria's? She saw a tear in Austin's eye as he joined the children and knelt down to embrace them. Rebecca stood watching the family as the wind whipped at her neatly placed hair. She tucked a loose tendril back into the pins but to no avail. She gave up and concentrated on the scene before her.

"Is this where Mama is?" asked Kelly Anne.

"Her body is there but the real part of her is in heaven with Jesus," Austin answered softly.

"Why can't we see her, Papa?" Kristie asked.

"We can't see her, but we can talk to her. Do you want to do that?"

"Yes, Papa," Kristie said and the other girls nodded their heads in agreement.

"Go ahead then."

"Mama, I miss you," Kelly Anne said.

"I miss you, too, Mama, but Jesus sent us a new mama. She's nice just like you."

"And she's pretty just like you, too!" added Carrie.

"But, Mama, she's very sad. Maybe her Mama went to heaven, too."

Rebecca listened from a distance, not wanting to intrude and overwhelmed with her emotions, as well. Tears choked in her throat in sadness for the girls' loss. She was taken back at the realization that the children had sensed her own pain. She vowed to mask it better, but wondered if she could. Was she in mourning, as the   children were for their dead mother? Who had she lost? After a few moments of silence, it hit her. She gasped as she realized she was mourning for herself and for the death of her childhood that never was. Rebecca turned from the scene of the children before her. It was too much to bear. She began walking down the hill.

After talking to their mama, the girls ran down the hill after Rebecca. They called out to her, and she stopped walking and knelt down and hugged them. Tears flowed from her eyes for their loss and her own. Austin joined them and took the baby from Rebecca's arms. He took one of the girl's hand and she took the others, and hand-in-hand, they walked back to the little house Rebecca now called home.

~*~

That night Rebecca crawled into bed and thought about the day. Austin deserved a wife who could love him as Victoria had done. She did not think that she could be that person. He needed more than a nanny and a housekeeper. He needed a friend and a companion, someone who was excited to see him and shared his dreams.

Austin crawled in beside her, and as if sensing her mood, spoke softly to her, "Rebecca, you're doing a wonderful job with the children. I don't know what I would have done if you wouldn't have come when you did. You've got a big responsibility. I know," he chuckled, "I tried to do it by myself and failed miserably." He turned his back to her and pulled the light covering up over his shoulders.

Rebecca lay still, not giving him any sign of listening. Soon she heard his steady breathing of sleep and relaxed slightly. Her mind raced from the emotions that she had experienced during the day. It was a big responsibility, but she was doing a good job. Austin had admitted it to her. He really did need her and she needed to be needed by someone. Was that what made one's life have meaning? Was that what would help her find out who she was? Would that fill the emptiness in the very center of her being? If it would, she would work extra hard to make this the best home Austin had ever seen.

The next morning Rebecca awoke to find Austin gone already. Had he forgotten his promise to go into town? Rebecca was disappointed, but went to work on her morning chores. Shortly Austin returned to the house.

"Ready to go?" he asked as he entered the kitchen.

Rebecca spun around and looked at him, "I...thought you weren't going since you weren't here when I came out."

"I promised you didn't I?"

"Yes," Rebecca said softly remembering promises not kept and even worse promises of bodily harm kept brutally.

She turned and went to get ready.

When the whole family was ready and in the wagon, Austin said, "Would you like a driving lesson?"

"I...I...don't know," Rebecca said lamely. She was not very good at learning new things. She knew that because her father had told her often that she was stupid.

"You'll need to know in case of an emergency or for times when I can't go into town with you. Come on, give it a try!"

Reluctantly, Rebecca handed the baby back to the girls and took the reins Austin offered her.

Austin put his hands on hers, and a chill went through her at his touch, but she did not reveal the emotions running through her.

"Now, hold the reins tightly but not too tight. They are what tells the horses what to do."

Austin went step by step through the directions, and Rebecca was surprised by the gentleness of his voice. Any instructions from her father began with him shouting and Rebecca quivering in fear. She realized that when instructions were given in kindness, she learned quickly.

She called to the horses and snapped the reins. With a gasp of surprise she felt the horses obey her. She concentrated on what she was doing and soon she was steering them out of the yard onto the road. She smiled with pleasure at the feel of the horses' obedience to her leading.

"You're doing a great job, Rebecca. You learn quickly."

His words were like a balm on Rebecca's soul.

She drove the wagon the whole way to town, and when they stopped in front of Mrs. Morgan's, she turned a beaming face toward her husband.

Austin grinned at her, "Thanks for the ride, Mrs. Finnigan!"

She blushed at the name and answered, "You're welcome."

"Why don't you go on in, and I'll take the children with me. You can meet me at the store when you're through. No need to rush. I'm sure Miles Conley will want to talk for a while. I probably disappointed him last week when I didn't stop to get filled in on all the town news."

Austin hopped down and helped Rebecca down from the wagon. She walked up the steps of the house. It was the first time she had been free of the family since she had arrived several weeks ago. She had a strange sense of being incomplete and turned to wave the family good-bye.

She knocked at the door and was greeted by Mrs. Morgan.

"Hello, dear, are you alone today?"

"Yes," replied Rebecca shyly.

"Come inside and see if the garments will fit," Mrs. Morgan said with an encouraging smile.

Rebecca followed the plump woman to the next room and watched as she retrieved the garments. Rebecca gasped at their beauty as Mrs. Morgan laid them out for her to see. She did not expect the intricate detail on the bodice of the dress. Little flowers had been embroidered down the front, running along the buttons going down the bodice. The sleeves were puffy and full. The dress looked so dainty.

"Now see the way the waist is with the pleats?" Mrs. Morgan pointed out. "There's room to grow there." She smiled with a twinkle in her eye. The way she spoke made Rebecca place her hand on her stomach lovingly.

"Here's the wool dress. It is not pretty, but it will be quite warm this winter."

Rebecca looked at the dress and matching cape and admired the neat small stitches, "It is beautiful, too." she said, "Thank you so much for doing the work for me."

Mrs. Morgan beamed with pride over Rebecca's words.

After trying on the dresses and finding them to be a perfect fit, Mrs. Morgan said, "Would you like to sit down for a cup of tea?"

Rebecca hesitated. Would Austin be expecting her? He did say to take her time, and since she did not need to be refitted, she decided it was alright to stay.

Rebecca nodded her acknowledgment of the invitation, and Mrs. Morgan led her into the sitting room. She excused herself but returned quickly and placed a tray before Rebecca with a tea pot, cups, sugar, cream, and a plate full of cookies.

"Thank you, Mrs. Morgan," Rebecca said as she accepted the cup of steaming tea from her hostess.

"Oh, please call me Emma, I have a feeling we're going to be good friends."

Rebecca looked at her in surprise. Mrs. Morgan, Emma, wanted to be her friend.

"So you're from Ireland, are you?" Emma asked as she offered Rebecca sugar and cream.

"Yes, I have only been in America a few months."

"Really? I came from England twenty years ago," she said with a starry look in her eyes. "Would you like to hear about it?" Rebecca nodded, grateful that she did not have to keep up her side of a conversation.

Emma smiled and began, "I was living in London. My mother and I worked day and night as seamstresses to keep food on the table for her and myself. My father had died when I was ten, and my mother and I had fought to keep a roof over our heads. Now, I'm grateful for those years of learning how to sew, but then I dreamed of leaving and finding a husband to sweep me away from the poverty that seemed to be waiting for us outside our door."

Rebecca blushed at the memory of her dreams of a young man coming to rescue her from her own suffering.

"Then my mother received a letter from her sister here in America. She said that there were not many young girls here for the men to marry. She had made arrangements, if I was willing, to be married to a man in their church. He was willing to take in my mother, as well, if she desired to come along."

Her face lit up as if she was that eighteen year old again and not the gray haired plump woman.

"My prince was waiting for me in America. We did not even have a second thought. Mother was excited about seeing her sister again and so she wrote back to say yes. The man, my dear George, sent us tickets and we were off. The voyage was rough and I was fearful for Mama's health. But she longed so for her sister that I think it kept her going."

Emma stopped to offer Rebecca a cookie and then continued, "I was very nervous when I saw my aunt standing at the docks with a man. I could not bear to look at him. What if he was ugly? What if he was not what I expected my prince to look like? After Mama and Aunt Harriett had embraced and said their hellos, Harriett introduced George to us. I just couldn't look at him," she chuckled at the memory of her nervousness. "I just looked at his boots. They were all clean and shiny, by the way."

"'Nice to meet you, Miss Sloan,' came a voice so booming that I looked up in surprise into the gentlest face I had ever seen. Then I knew that it wasn't a strikingly handsome man that I envisioned, but a kind man. And he was not bad looking, either!" she laughed.

Rebecca smiled at her. It was hard to picture the older woman as one who was young and looking for a beau.

"Well, we got married that very day! I was so nervous, but he was so kind to me, and well, we had three boys and two girls, to prove our love for each other! Now, all of them have gone farther west, and Mama and George have gone to be with the Lord."

"You're all alone!" Rebecca said without thinking.

"Oh, I have my friends, the church, and my customers. But best of all, I have the Lord to be with me."

Rebecca sensed the peace in the woman's voice and smiled, wishing she could have that same feeling. Rebecca stood to go, knowing that she needed to meet Austin. "Thank you so much, for the tea and the story, Mrs., I mean Emma."

Emma took Rebecca's hand, "You and I are quite alike. We did not know the men we married much before our wedding days. But it will work out for you, just like it did for me. I just know it. Austin is a nice, Godly man. He will be good to you. I can tell."

A tear came to Rebecca's eye. How did Emma know what was happening in Rebecca's life: a loveless marriage she was destined to endure for the rest of her days?

"I did not love my husband at first sight, but I grew to love him with each kind act he showed to me and my mother," Emma said, as if reading Rebecca's mind.

Rebecca pondered the older woman's words as she carried her packages to meet her family. Emma had grown to love her husband. Could she grow to love hers? Well, Emma's husband was different. He did not have a first wife who he missed and wished would not have died. Rebecca ached with the knowledge that Austin desired another woman. She was not good enough to compete for his love.

Rebecca was quiet on the ride back to the farm and even declined the offer to drive. Austin wondered what had caused the change and hoped that it was only from tiredness.

Chapter 13

Rebecca spent the remainder of the week working extra hard to meet the children's needs and keep up with things. The soreness in her body seemed to fade and she knew that she was getting used to the labor. She still fell exhaustedly into bed each night, but always with a sense of accomplishment. She was helping Austin to make a home for his children and a home for her and her baby. She might not be able to earn his love, even if she wanted it, but she would prove to him that he needed her. Still, all her hard work was to no avail in filling the emptiness inside that threatened to overwhelm her at a moment's notice.

Another Sabbath came quickly. Austin had reminded her about the picnic following the service, and she had prepared several dishes to share with the other families. The Sabbath morning found Rebecca up before Austin. Finally, she could fulfill her duty, she thought. She began to gather logs for the fire, when he walked into the kitchen.

"Rebecca, that's my job."

She looked up at him and said, "I can do it!"

"Those logs are too heavy for you. I will make the fire each morning. That is my job."

He strode over to her, and took the logs from her and began stoking the fire. She reached over to the coffee pot and began to make the coffee. She jumped as she sensed Austin standing near her. She turned slightly toward him. He put his hand on her hand as she held the coffee pot, and she looked up at him in surprise. She went to step back from him but the sink was in the way. Now she was facing him but kept her head bowed down.

He smiled down at her, "And I like to make coffee in the morning. It's one thing I can do just for you to welcome you in the morning. I make the porridge for the children, but the coffee is for you. When you see it sitting there on the stove I hope it reminds you that I appreciate your sacrifice for us."

She looked up into his eyes and blinked back the tears that threatened to escape. She was overwhelmed by emotions that were new to her. She released her hand from the coffee pot and tried to turn from him. He did not move away. She looked back up at him, and he reached out his other hand and touched a thick ringlet laying on her shoulder. "I love your hair, Rebecca. I like it when it's down." Then he turned and began making the coffee. Rebecca slipped by him and stood at the shelves to get the oats for the porridge. She fought back the raging emotions his words had stirred and felt the rapid beating of her heart. She knew if she had to speak she would be hoarse from the emotion rising in her throat. This was not the usual emotion of fear she experienced when she was near a man. This felt warm and different. She touched the ringlet of hair he had touched and surprised herself with the thought of wishing she could reach out and touch him as well. She chided herself for thinking that the touch meant something significant and she did her best to shake off her feelings and prepared the simple breakfast.

She wore her new dress proudly, appreciating the man who had insisted on it being made and the kind woman who had made it. The church service did not seem so strange to Rebecca this week. She knew what to expect and was overjoyed when she remembered some of the words of the hymns. She heard Austin's strong voice beside her and felt a sense of comfort at how strong and sure of himself he was. She was surprised when the hymns were over, and he rose to share from the Bible. He talked about trusting God and suffering.

"I have realized in these past months that God does not promise us an easy way of life. When we give our lives to Him it does not mean that we will be spared loss or trouble." His voice cracked at the word "loss", but he did not hesitate for even a moment. He continued in his strong deep voice, "He says that very thing in His Word in John 16,'In the world you will have tribulation but be of good cheer I have overcome the world.' In the Psalms, I read, 'Cast your care on the Lord, for he will sustain you; He will never let the righteous fall.' I have come to realize that in those tribulations He sustains us, He gives us strength to go on, and His peace helps us to make it through. As the Apostle Paul said, 'I have learned to be content in every circumstance. I can do everything through him who gives me strength.' And so my dear friends, although I stumble and sometimes wonder where God is, He gently reminds me in His Word that He is right beside me in my darkest hour and my greatest need."

Rebecca absorbed every word that came from Austin's lips. She desired to have God near her in her need. She wished that she would have known Him back in Ireland. Would it have been easier for her and her mother if they had listened sooner to the woman who visited at the shop? Tears fell from Rebecca's eyes and splashed on to the sleeping baby in her arms.

Austin returned to his seat. Seeing her tears, he handed her his handkerchief and put his arm around her. She looked up at him and saw that peace on his face that he had described. That's what made him different! It was God's peace that drew her to him. That's why she didn't fear him like other men. She gave him a smile and bowed her head as the congregation was dismissed in prayer. Austin did not rise immediately, but gave Rebecca time to recover before he escorted her out into the sunshine.

They walked to the wagon to retrieve the food Rebecca had prepared. Rebecca reached out to pick up a plate, but Austin placed his hand upon hers. She looked up at his smiling face as he spoke.

"Rebecca, I felt that God had left me when He took Victoria from me. I did not know how I was going to go on. I felt bitterness and anger towards Him. I wondered how He could let that happen to me when I served Him and followed Him faithfully. For a long time, I wouldn't read His Word. Prayer seemed to stick in my throat."

Rebecca wanted to reach up and touch his face and console him but held herself back.

"That day you came to the house to offer to help us, I was still angry and bitter. But even in that anger I felt God saying, 'Here's what I have brought for you. I have not forsaken you.' And those days when you seemed so near death, I read from the Bible for the first time since Victoria had died. The words I read to you consoled me in my loss and strengthened me even as they soothed your pain."

Rebecca remembered those words and how they had brought peace to her own tortured soul. Now she understood how they had affected him as well.

Austin went on, searching her eyes for the acceptance he desired from her, "I knew that I could never again stop reading the Bible. It is one of the things God uses to give us strength. I know that these last weeks have been rough for you, but I wanted you to know that I really am grateful for God's provision when He sent you to us. I hope and pray that you will receive from us what you need. Just as we have been blessed by you."

Austin reached his hand up and wiped the tears from Rebecca's eyes. She closed them and allowed his hand to remain on her cheek and felt a peace come over her.

Austin longed to lean down and kiss her tears away, but dared not. He chuckled and she opened her eyes as he took a wild strand of hair and twisted the ringlet around his finger saying, "I so love your hair. I'm glad that it doesn't listen to you and stay in the pins."

She smiled at him and could sense an electrical charge in the air between them. Her feelings for him were growing, but she was unsure of how to react. She did not want to turn away from him so she placed her hand on his chest. Their eyes met, and time seemed to stand still as they gazed at each other. Neither one wanted to break the feeling between them.

A lusty cry from Ryan in Rebecca's arms shocked them into awareness of their surroundings, and Rebecca took her eyes from Austin and shifted the baby into another position.

Austin turned and gathered up the food, and they walked toward the waiting tables in silence.

Rebecca went to feed the baby and was grateful for the few minutes to collect her thoughts before she joined the women. What were these feelings that she had just experienced? She did not know but she knew she liked them. A flash of a moment she had seen Erin and Thomas together came to her mind.

She had come across them in the doctor's house standing close looking into each other's eyes. They were speaking in whispers and were oblivious to her and their surroundings. She had watched them for a few seconds and then quickly turned so as not to disturb them. Still, she had seen enough to long for whatever it was they had. Something told her now that the feelings she was having for Austin matched those that moment.

Rebecca finished taking care of the baby and then joined the group of women standing at the tables. Mrs. White introduced her to each woman that she had not met yet. Emma Morgan was there and walked over to give her a huge hug.

"It's good to see you, dear. How are you and your little family?"

"Fine. Austin loves the clothes you made me."

"I knew he would. A man always loves to see a pretty woman all dressed up," she said as she winked.

Rebecca gasped at the words, "pretty woman."

Mrs. White smiled, as if reading her mind, "Yes, dear you are a pretty one! Hasn't anyone told you that?"

Rebecca's thoughts went back again to the names her father called her. Ugly was one that was extremely hurtful. The recent memory of Austin touching her hair put a smile on her face. At least Austin liked her hair, she thought as her hand unconsciously went to her face and she twisted a ringlet in her fingers. Her musings were interrupted by the call to eat.

Everyone gathered around the tables heavy laden with delectable foods. Mr. White prayed for the meal. Austin came and took Ryan from Rebecca. She found little Kelly Anne filled a plate for her and herself.

It was hard to choose what to put on the plate. There was food from several nationalities on the table, and she found herself sampling recipes she had never tasted before. After the meal, the women gathered, and much to Rebecca's joy, they shared their recipes.

The women's talk consisted of advice to the younger women with ideas to make their work easier, stories about their children, news from their homeland, and concern and prayers for their crops.

Rebecca did not get a chance to speak with Austin again, but she found herself constantly searching the crowd for him. To her surprise, she seemed to meet his gaze whenever she spotted him. She longed to be near him again and listen to his strong voice. She realized this desire was new, over the past weeks when she had been grateful for his long hours in the fields and barn. She remembered how on the ship Erin could not wait each morning to get dressed and meet Thomas out on the deck. She recognized the same anticipation in her own feelings and was surprised. Was she falling in love with Austin? She could not believe that it would be possible. If she was, it was far more than she had expected.

The words, "In God's hands," came to her mind. Did God not only want to take care of her, but give her true love also? She wanted to know more about God and hoped that she would learn in church what she needed to better understand Him and His plans.

Finally, the time came for the families to head back for the evening chores. Austin arrived at her side to help carry the empty plates back to the wagon and round up the children. He handed Ryan to her and his hand brushed her arm as she took the baby. His touch tingled, and she looked up at him to meet his grin. He could sense the change in her and reveled in the hope that she was no longer afraid of his touch.

He lifted her up into the wagon and helped the sleepy girls up, too. He swung up beside her, took the reins, and whistled for the bay to go. Then he pulled Rebecca close to him and began whistling. Austin was pleased when Rebecca did not pull away from him but instead laid her head on his shoulder and sighed with contentment.

~*~

The following week's routine was broken with a visit from Mrs. White. She swept into the house and chirped at how well kept it was and how good the children looked and acted.

"Why, just a month without a mama can make a child seem lost, but you've brought them around to their happy little selves again!" she declared.

Rebecca looked at her questioningly.

"Why honey, you should have seen these children that month after Victoria passed on. They didn't play, they didn't smile, they just clung to Austin, and he wasn't much better than they were. He lost a lot of weight, and he didn't seem to care much about anything. I think taking care of the young'uns overwhelmed him.

But I noticed a big difference in all of them after you came. Why, at the picnic on the Sabbath, the children were off running and playing with the other children, and my John even said that Austin was boasting about his new wife to the other fellas."

Rebecca blushed at the thought of Austin boasting about her, and a warm sense of pride welled up in her breast. He really did mean what he had said to her. She was making a difference in their lives. Was it possible that his appreciation could grow into love for her? The thought was more than she could hope for.

~*~

The days grew shorter, and Austin felt the pressure of getting ready for the harvest. He was thankful that it had been a good summer with just the right amount of rain. The crops were doing well.

Rebecca settled into her own routine. The girls' company and daily laughter seemed to fill the air, bouncing off the walls and ceilings to embrace Rebecca and heal her heart. She soon began to laugh openly at the baby's cute expressions or the girls' antics, but she never laughed in Austin's presence.

She had never dreamed that it was possible to truly feel happy and secure. She had never laughed as a child and reveled in the way the joy flowed from her at a whim. Although she knew without a doubt that Austin was different than her father, there was still a part of her that she could not shake; the fear that had been ingrained in her since a child. Her emotions were such a contradiction: a fear of her husband and a desire for him.

As a child, she had never been alone much to sit in peace or play. Her father was always there. Even though that life was behind her now, she still could not sit idly for a moment and found herself working from the time she rose until she collapsed into bed at night. Her desire was to please Austin. As a child she had worked constantly to please her father trying to earn his favor. But it was always in vain.

But with Austin it was different. He showed his appreciation in a smile, in an encouraging word, in the coffee and fire waiting for her each morning, and above all in the respect he showed her in their physical relationship. With all the encouragement he gave her, she still felt uneasy around him. He never saw the joy that the girls had the privilege of experiencing.

One day in early fall, however, the girls convinced her to come out to play. With no pressing work to be found, Rebecca reluctantly gave in to their begging. She carried the baby out to the porch in his basket as he slept.

Austin returned to the house earlier than usual that day. While coming around the corner he heard the children giggling and laughing. He stopped short when he heard the most pleasing sound he had heard in months, Rebecca laughing along with his girls. He peeked around the corner to see the girls and Rebecca playing in the yard. He didn't want to disturb them, but it was too late. Carrie had spotted him. She ran to him and dragged him to the circle, and he joined hands with the girls. At first, Rebecca paused at his presence but when she saw the joy in his eyes-when she saw his love for his children-finally she let her fears go. The entire family continued to laugh and giggle as they played their silly imaginative game. Austin saw sparkles in Rebecca's eyes as they twirled around in the circle and sang the silly song the girls had invented. Her cheeks were rosy from the wind and the laughing. Austin could not take his eyes away from her beautiful face.   When the game was over, the girls started hugging Rebecca. Austin joined them. He picked Rebecca up and swung her around, holding her tight. She continued to laugh as Austin stumbled slightly and the pair landed on the ground.

The girls jumped on top of them. Rebecca's sweet laugh tickled Austin's funny bone and he began laughing uncontrollably. The whole family lay on the ground laughing and hugging each other.

Rebecca felt completely free for the first time in her life. As she laughed, she felt the depression and grief that hung over her lift. She laughed and rolled on the ground until Austin sat up and pulled her closer. She looked into his eyes. A feeling of complete security filled her being. He saw in her eyes what he had for so long desired. He paused for a moment then he leaned forward and kissed her.

Rebecca was surprised by the kiss but not afraid of it. She did not pull away from him, but kissed him in return. As she did, her breath caught in her throat as she felt the longing for him course through her. She reached up and wrapped her arms around his neck. It was as if the moment stood still.

Just as quickly as the kiss came, it ended when one of the girls tackled the pair back down onto the ground. They lay there for a few moments just looking into each other's eyes, saying nothing with words but volumes with looks.

Little Ryan began crying from the porch. Rebecca broke her gaze to look over at the baby. She tried to get up from the ground and laughed when Austin would not let her go. Finally, when Ryan would not stop crying, Austin hopped up and extended his hand to Rebecca. She accepted gratefully, and he effortlessly pulled her to her feet. He pulled her to himself and kissed her forehead. He smoothed the tiny ringlets that had escaped back from her face, then he compulsively reached behind her head and pulled the pins out letting her ringlets cascade down her back. At his touch, she lost all sense of her surroundings and closed her eyes, reveling in his gentleness, surprised at her acceptance of his nearness. She wanted the embrace to last forever. So did Austin. They hardly noticed as Carrie went to baby Ryan and quieted him.

The children ran off to play with the baby as their parents stood in the yard oblivious to the world around. Austin kissed

Rebecca's closed eyes tenderly. Rebecca wrapped her arms around her husband's waist desiring to get as close as she could to him. He continued to kiss her eyes, and her cheeks. Rebecca lifted her lips and sought his out. This time the kiss lasted until each had communicated their full desire for the other.

Austin pulled his lips from hers as Ryan gave another lofty cry for attention. Austin and Rebecca laughed. It seemed Ryan was always crying at the most inopportune times. Rebecca released her arms from around her husband, and they walked arm in arm to the porch. She reluctantly let go of his arm and picked up the baby. She held him and looked at Austin. He reached out and brushed pieces of grass from her hair. He cupped her face in his hand and kissed her again. The baby began to whimper, and Rebecca knew that this special moment had come to an end. She needed to change his diaper and feed him. She reluctantly turned, pleasantly assured that it was only the first of many more moments like it to come.

Chapter 14

That night Austin crawled into bed beside Rebecca with anticipation: he did not turn his back toward her but cradled her in his arms from behind.

She tensed with excitement, but he took it to mean that she was still not ready. So, he did not kiss her but continued to hold her through the night. He longed for her so, but had made a promise to her and to God to wait for her. It would be only by God's grace that he could do so. She felt a wave of disappointment when he did not repeat the events of earlier that day, but soon fatigue took over, and she slept soundly and dreamed of him.

The next day, Mr. White and his sons arrived to help Austin bring in the harvest. They worked all day and into the night with only a stop for a delicious meal prepared and served by a smiling Mrs. White and Mrs. Finnigan.

Mrs. White noticed immediately the new sparkle in Rebecca's eyes and the look she saw there when Austin came near.

"How are you and Austin doing these days?" she asked.

Rebecca blushed and looked down at the pie she was cutting. How could she answer that question without giving away the beating of her heart at the mention of his name? "Fine," she said blushing deeper at the lie. They were doing better than fine.

Mrs. White whispered a prayer of thanks to the Lord for putting the two together. For the next week the two families helped each other in their harvesting with Mrs. White's ever watchful eye on the little family.

When all the harvest was in the barns or safely transported to buyers in town, the family joined together to celebrate. They all stood around the table and joined hands. Austin's deep voice boomed his thanks to his God, "Lord, we thank Thee for sending good weather this summer. We thank Thee for this harvest. We thank Thee for the good prices we received for our crops. Best of all Lord, we thank Thee for our families and the love Thou has shown us." Austin squeezed Rebecca's hand so that she knew the prayer was for her. "Lord, bless us this winter. Keep us safe and especially look after Rebecca and the little life she carries within her. Bless the birthing," Austin's voice cracked with emotion at the memory of the last birth he attended, "Let no harm come to baby or mother. Amen."

Rebecca looked up as Austin turned from the group, but not before she saw him wipe a tear from his eye. She wanted to take him in her arms and tell him it would be okay, but she didn't. She had no words of encouragement from God's Word like he would have had for her. She did not know God well enough to know if He would grant Austin's request. She didn't want Austin to be hurt again like he had been at Victoria's death. She sighed at her inability to comfort him in his need, and turned to the table full of food, serving the men and then the children.

Once all the farmers had their crops safely harvested, it was time for a large community celebration. They planned an all-day event at the church. The women spent days baking, and early on a Saturday morning, they loaded the wagons with children and yields of the harvest and rode to the church.

Rebecca truly enjoyed the companionship of the other women. She never had a friend as a child, and she and her mother rarely found time to converse. She enjoyed the stories and each woman's personality in her new community. She was beginning to see the diversity in God's creation as each woman's uniqueness contributed to the group.

Her appreciation for the individuals she had met made her think about her own uniqueness. God had made her the way she was for a reason. Just as she accepted each woman, Mrs. White and her mother hen tendencies, Mrs. McHaney and her complaining attitude, and Mrs. Mooring and her incessant talking, so God also accepted each one. The women were created by Him and He loved and accepted them just as they were. Startled, but pleased at the thought, Rebecca realized that God had accepted her, too. He loved her despite her quirks and past failures. If He was happy with who she was, SHE could, be too.

When she first arrived in town she did not know who she was or what she liked, but now she knew that she enjoyed cooking, loved to play with the children, and hated doing laundry. She realized that she liked her personality. She found herself humming or singing the hymns from church all through the day and very rarely got angry or disappointed. She reflected on the day of the visit to the creek. She hadn't felt free to let go and be herself. She had pushed down her emotions to cover her feelings. She realized that she could live in fear and sadness over the past or she could finally allow herself to relax in her own skin. That past, though painful, had developed endurance and patience which fit her well now on the prairie where hard work and disappointments were the norm.

She also realized that it was okay to allow positive emotions to shine through. She looked forward to seeing Austin during the brief moments when she joined the girls to carry his lunch to him. She relished feeling his strong arms around her in bed at night. She longed for more moments with him. It was a new and thrilling experience.

Still, though she was gaining a sense of this new self-discovery, something was still missing. There was an emptiness in the center of her being that could not be touched or filled even with Austin's laughter or a hug and kiss from one of the children.

It seemed that she came closest to filling the void on Sunday mornings when she sang the songs about God and listened to the reading of the Word. But even those things never completely filled the emptiness. Some nights that pain and loneliness overwhelmed her, and she would cry silently. She closed her eyes at the memory.

After a moment, she brought herself back to the chatter of the women around her and met Mrs. White's eyes. The older woman looked at her with concern. Had her face revealed the turmoil within her? Rebecca wondered. Mrs. White leaned forward and took Rebecca's hand.

"Come, dear, help me get some water."

Rebecca obeyed and followed her to the pump. Rebecca pumped the handle as the cool water splashed around the hem of her dress.

"Are you feeling okay, dear?" Mrs. White asked gently, gesturing at Rebecca's swollen stomach.

"I'm feeling fine. I'm carrying the baby well. It's not that," she said, hesitating to put into words what was on her heart.

"Are you happy?" Mrs. White said boldly.

Rebecca smiled weakly, "I love living with Austin and the children." She did not feel able to convey the true feelings hidden in her heart.

"But there's more, isn't there?"

A tear fell from Rebecca's eye. This was not the place or the time to share her hidden pain, but she could not lie to Mrs. White. "Yes, but I can't speak of it." Rebecca's eyes pleaded with her dear friend to allow the issue to go.

"Okay, my dear, but you know where I am if you need my help, and you'll be in my prayers."

Rebecca sighed with relief as Mrs. White took the water and returned to the other women. Rebecca yearned to be able to talk to her but instead, trusted in those words that she was in "God's hands."

~*~

With the harvest in, Rebecca looked forward to seeing more of Austin throughout the day. She was disappointed when he still found a lot of daily work to do. However, they did have more time in the evenings to spend together. They put the children to bed and sat before the fire. Austin would read to Rebecca from the Bible as she sat sewing or mending the children's clothes.

Rebecca listened intently to the words about Jesus. She looked forward each day to the time she and Austin spent alone reading the Bible. She yearned to learn about this God who she knew made Austin different than the other men in her life, the God she knew without a doubt had rescued her from the terror of her life in Ireland and provided a new life for her.

As Austin read, Rebecca sympathized with the pregnant Mary traveling to a strange place. As he read of Jesus's healing ministry, she longed to be touched by Jesus's hand and be healed by Him. She found herself being angry at those desiring to kill Him, and she wept at His crucifixion. She was completely surprised at the story of His resurrection and rejoiced when He showed Himself to His followers.

For Austin their nightly readings were refreshing, too. He had heard the Scriptures since he had been a child, and although he loved them, he began seeing them anew through Rebecca's eyes.

It was after the reading of Christ's sacrifice on the cross that Rebecca realized that maybe God himself would fill the void, the emptiness in her life. She looked up at Austin and in a rare moment of disclosure said, "I feel empty inside. I want to be happy, but I'm not. I love living here and enjoy it, but there's something missing. Tell me, Austin, why can't I find peace?" She began to weep and placed her head in her hands.

Her shoulders shook as sobs from deep within wracked her body.

Austin immediately joined her and wrapped his arms around her. "Rebecca, the answer is Jesus Christ. He made each one of us to have that emptiness that can only be filled by Him."

"But, I pray, and I go to church. What else am I supposed to do?" she sobbed.

"Remember in the book of John when we read about being born again?"

She shook her head, yes, and he went on, "That's what needs to happen to you. Do you want to be born again?"

She shook her head again, and he said, "You just tell the Lord that you want Him to live inside of you and be a part of your life. You tell Him that you want Him to be your Lord. That means to be your leader. Tell Him that you want to listen to His commands."

"Oh, Austin, I do, I do want Him. But does He want me? There is so much inside of me, so much anger and fear, why would He want me?"

"He won't turn anyone away that comes to Him, and He'll take that anger away. He says in the Bible, 'Fear not for I am with you,' and 'I will never leave you nor forsake you.' He's waiting for you Rebecca. Will you ask Him in tonight?"

"But, Austin, you don't understand. I have done things that I don't think He can forgive."

"There is nothing that He can't forgive. What could you have possibly done that He could not forgive? It is what others have done to you that I have a hard time forgiving."

"Oh, Austin, but, I...I...,"

"Rebecca, tell me. Why are you so fearful?"

Rebecca looked away from her new husband. How could she tell him? What if he rejected her? Austin took her face in his hand and looked into her eyes, "Nothing you could have done would make me abandon you. I love you."

Rebecca looked at him in surprise. He loved her! She began to cry again. He took her into his arms tightly and whispered to her, "I love you, Rebecca Finnigan. Nothing will stop me from doing so!"

Rebecca could hardly believe her ears. This Godly, good, kind man LOVED her. It was more than she could bear. How could she ever confess her dark past to him now?

She pushed him away trembling, and said, "But Austin, I...my...oh...it's so hard to say." She turned her face away from his and continued, "On my wedding night Richard died. I killed him!"

"Oh, darling, that's not possible, you're such a snip of a girl."

"Well, when I woke up he was dead! He... oh Austin it was so awful! I did not know him until the day my father made me marry him. He looked to be the same age as my father, and he was so mean. It was awful." Her eyes grew big with fear, "He ripped my dress, he hit me, he...." Rebecca sobbed unable to say the words.

"It's okay, darling, it's okay. I know what happened. I wish I could have been there to rescue you."

"But, Austin, you don't understand. I killed him!"

"Rebecca, what do you mean?"

"He...he...kept waking up and..." She couldn't say the words. "When he finally stopped, I was afraid to move. I just lay there. When hours went by and there was no response from him, I touched him and...and he was cold. He was dead! I killed him!"

Austin looked at her wide eyes of fear and regret and wanted to smile. She was so beautiful. "Darling, you did not kill him. He was old. His heart probably could not take it anymore. He just died."

"But, Austin," she protested. He did not seem to understand.

"No, Rebecca, I know without any doubt that you did not kill him. He was the one that chose to be cruel to you. He caused his own death. You were just a victim of his cruelty."

~*~

Anger filled Austin's eyes as he too thought about the horror that night must have been for Rebecca. Rebecca mistook his emotion as anger towards her, and she shirked away. Just as quickly as the anger came, it left, and Austin reached out for Rebecca. At his touch, she began to scream, "No, no, don't hurt me!"

"Rebecca, Rebecca," he said firmly, "I would never hurt you. It is him I'd like to hurt for doing this to you!"

"Oh, Austin, I thought you'd hate me for it. I couldn't bear to tell you. I feel so ashamed, so dirty."

"Oh, my sweet Rebecca, I could never hate you. It was not your fault. Come, let me hold you."

Rebecca moved toward him, and he took her in his arms.

"I want to be free of this pain. I know I need God to help. I want Jesus to be in my life. How do I do it?" Rebecca said into Austin's ear.

"Just say these words after me, "Lord Jesus..." Austin led Rebecca in a simple prayer of need and commitment. Afterward a few moments, she fell to her knees and clung to Austin. Indescribable peace washed over her in that moment. She could feel God's presence in a new way.

"Oh, Austin, I'm so glad that I came to live with you. I would have never met you, and the children, and Jesus, if I hadn't."

Together they wept tears of joy over Rebecca's new found peace and clung to each other for a long time before they silently retired to bed.

Rebecca awakened the next morning with a deep sense of peace. She joined Austin in the kitchen with a smile on her face. He looked up from the table and smiled at her, "You look different today."

"I feel different today."

Austin held out his hands toward her, and she readily accepted them. He stood up and pulled her to himself. "Dear Lord, we thank Thee for the mighty work Thou has done in Rebecca's heart. Lord, continue to help her and show her Yourself as she reads Your Word. Amen."

"Amen," Rebecca echoed and looked into her husband's eyes. Their eyes locked and Rebecca's heartbeat quickened. Oh, how she loved this man who had showed God's unconditional love to her. How could she ever show him how much she appreciated him?

Austin's gaze left her eyes and looked at her thick red lips, parted ever so slightly. How he longed to kiss them. Did he dare? He looked back at her eyes to find them closed. He kissed them. Rebecca tightened her hold on him. She had thought that once he had heard about Richard he would be repulsed by her and was relieved to find that it wasn't true. He could hear her breath quicken at the touch. She seemed to go weak as he held her tightly. He kissed her cheek and was about to kiss her on the mouth when he heard giggling from behind her. He looked up to find the girls in their nightgowns standing before them.

The spell was broken, and Rebecca opened her eyes. She turned to look at the girls and then back at Austin. She giggled at the fact that they were always being interrupted by one of the children. Then she turned to help the girls get dressed.

Chapter 15

One evening Rebecca found Austin standing in the bedroom looking at the bureau full of Victoria's clothes. He looked up at her and smiled, "It's about time we go through her things and make room for yours."

"I have a place for my things," she said referring to the satchel she had never truly unpacked.

"You're here to stay. It is time you put your things away properly. When I see you getting things out of that satchel I feel as if you are here just temporarily. You're not are you?"

"No, Austin, I'm here to stay," she answered confidently.

He smiled and turned to open a drawer. "It would not bother me if you wore some of her things. I know you could use more clothes. We did not have much time to get you many things before we got busy with the harvest."

He emptied each drawer gently onto the bed and looked at it all.

He stood quietly, and Rebecca placed her hand on his arm, saying, "I know you still miss her, Austin. It's okay. I understand."

"It's not that I don't love you, Rebecca. But Victoria and I had children together. I...I...." Austin began to cry.

Rebecca put her arm around him and drew him to herself, "I understand, Austin, honest I do. I would not expect you to stop grieving for her."

"Oh, Rebecca, I love you, so! What would I have done without you?"

Rebecca was surprised again at Austin's pledge of love to her. Could she say those words back to him? She wanted to do it, but something stopped her. Was it fear of being hurt or rejected? He had pledged his love to her. Was it not enough? She had even told him about Richard, and he still loved her.

He turned toward the items on the bed and began sorting through them. He found some jewelry alongside the clothes. There was a broach that Austin explained had been given to her by her mother the day they left Ireland, a delicately carved brush and mirror set, and a dainty necklace.

"I gave her the necklace the day the twins were born. I wanted her to know that I loved her and appreciated the sacrifice she made for the girls. I will save the jewelry to give to the twins and the brush and mirror set for Kelly Anne. I wish I had something for Ryan," he said, wrapping each of the items in Victoria's handkerchiefs.

"I know!" he said as he strode to his own dresser. He searched in one drawer for a few moments and then retrieved a coin.

"Her father gave me this gold coin and told me to not spend it unless I had an emergency. It seemed that there was never a big enough emergency to give up this gift."

Rebecca smiled at him, "I'm glad that the children each have something in remembrance of their mother."

Rebecca went through the clothes and chose the ones that she could wear. She picked up her satchel and placed it on the bed. She pulled out the two tattered dresses.

"Let's throw those away," Austin said softly.

"We can use them for rags," she smiled back at him.

A grin formed on her face as she pulled out the trousers and shirt she had worn to sneak on the ship.

"What are those for?" Austin asked.

"Well, I think I need to tell you the whole story of how I came to live here."

Austin sat down on the bed and pulled Rebecca down beside him and gave her his full attention. Rebecca almost lost her nerve at his attentiveness.

"Well, my mother and I were praying for a way of escape from Father. He was getting drunk more often, he was never happy with what I did, and every time he got drunk, he took it out on me." Rebecca's voice faltered as she remembered the last beating her father had given her. Austin placed his hand on hers and urged her to go on.

"I had dropped something, and it had spilled all over. He beat me for that mistake, and then later that night he beat me so bad that I thought I would die. Whenever I ruined anything in the store it meant that I did not eat that night. I was so hungry and so tired."

"That's why the day you dropped the bread you were so frightened?"

"Yes, I was very clumsy and missed a lot of meals. That night I stole an apple from the store and ate it. I knew if I didn't take care of myself that I could starve to death."

"You were probably clumsy because you were weak from hunger. Did that ever occur to you?"

"No, I never truly thought about why I did such things. I just knew I was a stupid clumsy girl that caused my father trouble."

"So, why did he beat you the second time?"

"I fell asleep in the store. He had left me there, and I was so tired, I could not stay awake. He came home drunk and found me there sleeping. It was the worst beating he had ever given me. That night I looked in his eyes, and I knew that he would and could kill me if more opportunities arose. The next day while he was sleeping, a woman came to the store and prayed with Mama that I would be able to leave. Well, not long after that Richard came. He had to be the same age as my father or older. My father told me he was to be my husband. I wondered if this was my way of escape, but I was very afraid and did not want to go. But Father had a minister come to the house that evening, and I was married. I took my belongings and followed him out to a waiting cab. We went to a hotel and then..."

"I had thought when you first came that you were distant because you grieved for your husband. I didn't realize all that you had gone through. What happened after he died?"

"I looked in his jacket and found the boat tickets and the money. I...I...took the tickets and some of the money. I stole them from him!"

"You were his wife! They now belonged to you!"

"But...but...."

"No, Rebecca, no buts, you had every right to them. So, what did you do next?"

"Well," she smiled, "I was afraid someone would stop me when I tried to get on the ship as a girl traveling alone, so I bought boy's clothes and dressed like a boy. I almost cut my hair off that day," she said teasingly.

"Oh no, I would not have been able to bear that," he said as he reached up and tugged at a stray tendril.

"On the ship, I felt so free and yet so lonely. I missed Mama, but I knew there was no other choice. Then I realized that God had made the way of escape for me. Not too long after that your sister came up to me and said, 'You're not a boy!'"

Austin laughed, "Mama, said she was a bold one!"

"Before I knew what was happening I had invited Erin to share my cabin with me. She was in with the general passengers and did not like it. Everyone was crammed together, and the crying of babies and the sea sickness kept her awake at night."

Austin's face changed to regret. Rebecca saw the change and quickly said, "It's okay, Austin. She said that you must not have realized what it was like for her, or you would have sent her a better ticket."

"So, she convinced me that it was safe to dress like a girl and gave me a dress of her own to wear. We were up on deck when we found that Thomas had followed Erin on board. Your sister was so smitten with him. It was not long before he asked her to marry him. That's when she decided that I could come and help you and Victoria with the children in her place. She was sure it was the best thing for me and for you."

"It was!" Austin interrupted.

"Well, you didn't think that at first!"

"I was just grieving for Victoria and mad at God."

"You were going to send me away!"

"Well, I would have, but you fainted at my feet!"

"I had a horrible trip on the train. I was so sick from being pregnant, but I didn't know that then. I didn't think about anything but getting here and resting."

"How did your dress get singed?" Austin said remembering vividly the day she came to the house.

"The train stopped suddenly and the fire spilled out onto the floor catching the dress of one of the girls on fire. I did not think for even a second, but threw myself on top of her to put it out."

Austin touched her face, "Oh, my little hero, no wonder you passed out when you got here. You had a rough time of it."

"I had only enough strength to get to your house and offer my services. When you said you didn't need me, it was too much for me. I had no more strength to continue."

"I'm sorry for putting you through that," he said soberly, "But if you hadn't fainted, we might not be together today."

"Those first few months were so hard. I was so afraid of...of..."

"Of, me!"

"Yes, of you! I didn't know you very well!"

"I could not truly understand your fear, but I knew it was real, so the Lord gave me the grace to wait for you."

"That first night of our marriage I could not get out of my mind the memories of that night with Richard. I was so afraid, but when you never came to bed, I finally fell asleep. But the nightmares came. I awoke to find you by my bed speaking words of encouragement. I wanted to believe you, but it was too much for me all at once. When I awoke the next morning to find you had slept there all night, I was so touched."

"That was the moment that I knew I loved you!"

"You loved me then?"

"Yes, my darling. God gave me the love for you because of the commitment I made to Him and to you, to marry you."

"Austin, I did not know. I thought that you wanted Victoria, not me!"

"Oh, Rebecca, God sent you to me, to take away the hurt of losing Victoria. How could I not love you? You took care of me and of the children. Those first days, I watched you putting your whole self into taking care of us. Cleaning, leaving the bathtub waiting for me, baking the cinnamon rolls; how could I not love you?"

"I was afraid you'd send me away if I did not work hard."

"You did more than work hard. You showed a tenderness and love for us that melted our hearts and made the children love you so quickly!"

"I was so afraid. Nothing I did ever pleased Father. I assumed you were the same way. I thought all men were that way."

"I know those first months were hard. When you would make the slightest mistake, your eyes showed such fear! But I did not know what to do to reassure you that it was okay."

"I wanted to please you. I was afraid I would be sent away like father threatened to do all those years and finally did."

"I loved you unconditionally. Nothing you did or could do would stop that love."

"Oh, Austin," she hugged him. "It's just like God's love. I think the way you treated me showed me how God loved me, too. I remember the first day I realized that I was falling in love with you!" she teased.

"When?" he said, his curiosity peaked.

"The day at the wagon when you told me how much you needed me and that you loved my hair."

"I remember that day! Ryan sure interrupted that moment for me. When he cried, I was so disappointed."

"But, I wasn't ready. I still needed time. But that day you kissed me in the yard, I knew then that I loved you."

"I thought so," he said smiling at her." Austin did not ask about that night in bed when he felt her tense at his touch. She had needed time before they were to be intimate. He realized that the intimacy he desired was hard for her because of the night the baby was conceived. For now, knowing that she loved him was enough.

Rebecca stood up and took her undergarments out of the satchel in one bunch, slightly embarrassed for him to see them. She placed them in the empty drawer.

She looked in the satchel and saw the one remaining item laying at the bottom, "Austin," she said hesitating, "I have something else you didn't know about."

She pulled the wad of money out and showed it to him. "It's left over from what I took from 'him'," not able to say his name or the words 'husband'.

She continued, "I wanted to tell you about it. But, I...."

"You weren't sure if you were going to be safe here and saved it for an escape."

"Yes, but I now know the truth. I'm here for good. It's not much money, but I want to give it to you."

"It's your money, and you should use it for what you want."

"But I want you to know that I am committed to you and this family. I see it as our money now."

"I know that. Why don't we put it somewhere for safe keeping and when the time is right we'll know how to use it? Okay?"

"Okay," Rebecca said. She placed the money in with the keepsakes that Austin had put away for the children.

"I wish I had something for my little one to keep," she said sadly. "I didn't bring anything with me from my parents. My mother had nothing."

"You can give him your love and a happier home than what you had as a child. Above all you will give him the legacy of Christ's love! There is no better treasure than that!"

Rebecca stood above her husband and placed her hands on his shoulders, "I'm also giving him a father to love him!" She leaned down and kissed him on the forehead and then pulled him to herself and held him close, "Thank you, Austin, for making me a part of your life."

~*~

Rebecca felt very settled in her new home. She had her clothes neatly folded in the drawers of the bureau. She had told Austin all of her secrets. She had told him about the money that seemed to keep her distant from him. She seemed to love him and the children more and more each day. She continued to thank God for keeping her "in His hands."

One night Rebecca woke to crying. She quickly went to the children's room. Kelly Anne was sobbing with her eyes closed. Rebecca touched her forehead and was surprised to find her burning with fever. She called for Austin, and when he did not answer her, she went to their room. He was also laying in the bed drenched in sweat.

"Austin," she cried, "What's wrong?"

"I don't know," he moaned, "I ache all over. I have chills one minute and then I get so hot I can't stand it the next."

"Kelly Anne is sick, too!"

"Oh," he said trying to get out of bed. Rebecca protested, but he ignored her and stood up dizzily.

As he swaggered, Rebecca quickly helped him back into bed. She then went to get Kelly Anne and brought her to their bed and put her in beside her father. She quickly got a basin of cool water and began placing cool cloths on their heads.

It was a rough few days. Austin was unable to get out of bed, and Rebecca had all the chores to do. She dressed in her wool cape and her boy's trousers and boots and trudged out through the snow to the barn. The animals seemed not to notice the change in routine until she had tried to milk the cow. The cow did not like Rebecca's inexperienced hands, but did not move until she was done. Rebecca kissed her on the head and thanked her for being good. She was grateful that Austin had taught her the farm routine, in case of emergencies like these, and although it took her much longer than it took him, she had finished the job. Rebecca turned to leave the barn and was surprised at the storm that had started. She could not see the house, and fear gripped her. How would she get home? Determined to get back as quickly as possible to her sick family, she started off toward what she thought was the right way. The snow hit her in the face. She put her hand up to the wind and tried to look for a familiar sign. She could not get her bearings and turned to return to the barn. But after many steps she could not find it either. She panicked and began crying out for help.

Austin stirred from his feverish sleep and looked out the window. It was snowing again. He called for Rebecca. He knew he'd better tell her how to get to the barn without getting lost in the snow.

When she did not answer, fear gripped his heart. He tried to get up from the bed and fell to his knees. He crawled out to the kitchen to find the twins playing with the baby, "Where's your mama?" he asked trying to not alarm the girls.

They looked at him and ran over to him and helped him stand up and walk to the table, "Papa, you should be in bed. Mama went to the barn."

"Oh, no," he cried as he looked out the window and only saw the blanket of snow. He prayed for the strength that he needed and rose from his chair, fighting off the wave of dizziness that threatened to bring him to his knees again. He dressed in his coat and boots and grabbed a rope. He tied the rope to his waist and opened the door. The door pulled from his hand and flew back, banging against the wall. He moved forward and stood on the porch, closed the door, and tied the rope to a hook next to it.

He made his way to the barn. He had made those steps several times a day, but was surprised to find how much the wind blew him off course. Eventually he found the barn door. He was grateful for the rope. He opened the door, praying that Rebecca was inside.

"Oh, no," he cried when he saw that she was not there. He began to pray.

"Oh, Lord, I cannot bear to lose another wife. Please, Lord, spare her. Help me to find her!"

He left the barn hoping that he would come across her as he made his way back to the house. He knew that he would only find her by the grace of God.

Rebecca stumbled and fell. She feared for the baby's safety and wrapped the cloak closer around her stomach. She tried to get up and slipped, crying in pain as she hit her head on something. She felt for the object blocking her path and realized that it was the chopping block for the wood pile. At least she knew where she was. "Thank you, Lord. She grabbed onto the block and pulled herself up. Which way was the house from here? She cried in exasperation and called out again for help.

"Rebecca?" called Austin. Had he heard her call? Please, please, call out again.

"Help, Austin, Help!"

It was her! He followed the sounds of her voice until he practically stumbled over her sitting on the block crying. He grabbed her, and pulling the rope taut, he led her back to the house. They burst inside the warm room, and the twins ran to them, helping them off with their coats and boots.

Rebecca's teeth were chattering, and Austin wearily led her to the fire. He wanted to wrap her up in blankets but the dizziness over took him and he fell to the floor at her feet.

Austin awoke to find that the girls had taken care of them both. He was laying on the floor wrapped in blankets, and Rebecca was sleeping in the rocker. Her steady breathing put his fears at ease. He turned to see the girls. They ran over to him, "Papa, are you okay?"

"Yes, thanks to you girls. You did a great job. Is Mama, okay?"

"She was very cold but we wrapped her up, and she stopped chattering. She's sleeping now," Kristie informed her father.

"I fed baby Ryan," chimed in Kelly Anne who recovered quicker than her father from the fever.

Austin smiled at her, "Good job, Kelly Anne. Can you girls keep an eye on things?" His voice faltered as he began to tire again.

"Yes, Papa. Mama showed me how to take care of the fire, and we have lots of bread to eat," Carrie said.

"Bring me a drink of water, honey."

Carrie obeyed and brought him the drink. He drank quickly and then laid back down thanking God for his little family.

It was another day before Austin was on his feet again, and thankfully neither he nor Rebecca had suffered any injury from their day in the storm. Again God had provided.

Chapter 16

"Soon it will be Christmas," announced Austin to his little family sitting around the dinner table.

Rebecca's face turned white. Her memory of Christmas was not a happy one. She remembered long hours in the store and her father "celebrating" by going out at night to drink with his friends. She did not receive any Christmas presents and most often received bruises instead.

She was brought back to the present with the cheers of the children. Of course, their memories of Christmas had to be good ones. They had a loving father who would have seen to that. She did not know what other families did for Christmas, but she had always envied the children of the customers who had come into the shop to buy dolls, toys, and candy for them.

Later that evening when the children were asleep, Rebecca asked Austin about past Christmases in their home.

"Well, Victoria always spent lots of time making the children special gifts. The girls got dolls, new mittens, and candy. We would get some sort of tree, though they're not easy to find around here. We would read the Christmas story and sing carols.

"What do you think we should do this year?" Rebecca asked hesitantly.

"I don't know. What did your family do?"

"Well," Rebecca fought back the tears that seemed to come so quickly when she remembered her childhood home. "We closed the store on that day, and..."

Austin looked at her questioningly, noting the pain on her face. "I'm sorry, Rebecca, I shouldn't have asked." He stood up from his chair, strode over and knelt before her. "I'm so sorry that your childhood was filled with such cruelty and bad memories. I wish I could take the pain away."

Rebecca looked down at him with tears streaming down her face, and said, "Since that night I asked Jesus to be part of my life, I've had a lot of peace about my family, but sometimes a memory will resurface and the horror all floods in again."

Austin took her into his arms and held her, "Rebecca, we can make new memories for you to replace the bad ones. We will make this Christmas extra special so that in the years to come, when you think about the past, this Christmas will be the one you remember."

Rebecca began to weep even more. "Darling, what's wrong?" Austin said as he released her. He pushed her hair back from her face and wiped her tears with his handkerchief.

"I'm so happy living here with you. I...I...never thought that a family could be so happy. You're so kind to me, and all I am is a bother. I'm always crying and..."

"Shhh..." Austin said putting his finger to her lips, "I am glad you're here. You're not a bother. I thank the Lord every day for sending you to me."

"Oh, Austin," Rebecca cried as she reached out and touched his face. "What would I have done without you?"

Austin took her into his arms again and held her as she continued to cry. He stood, walked her to their bedroom and held her tight until she fell asleep.

. He continued to hold her in his arms, long after he knew that she was asleep. He prayed for her, that the Lord would heal her hurts. He prayed that He would give him wisdom as to how to help her. As he dozed off to sleep, he felt an assurance that he was doing what God wanted him to do, to love her, accept her, and patiently wait for her healing.

~*~

The next evening, after the children were all tucked in for the night, Rebecca and Austin began planning their Christmas.

"Did you want me to do the same things that Victoria did for the children?" Rebecca asked Austin.

"I want this Christmas to be new. Something created by you and me, something different from the past."

"It's okay, Austin, if you want to do it Victoria's way."

"Everything around us reminds me of Victoria. My memories with her are precious, but you are my wife now. You need to see this as your home and your family."

Rebecca smiled at him, "But, I don't know what to do to make Christmas special. It's all new to me."

"Well, I'll help you. We'll do it together. Hasn't anything come to mind?"

"Well, yes," she looked at him hesitantly. He smiled and took her hand across the table. "I know how important the story of Christ's birth is, and I wondered if we could have the children act out the story's parts."

"That's a wonderful idea. Then they will really know the significance of the story and maybe understand it a little bit more." Austin said smiling.

"The girls are old enough to make gifts for each other." Rebecca continued." I thought we could help them do that."

"That sounds good. I have scraps of wood in the barn. Maybe they could make blocks for the baby or something."

Rebecca was reminded of her own resources, "I have lots of material scraps they could use to make dolls or stuffed animals."

"We could make our own decorations for the tree. We could pop popcorn and string them." Austin imagined aloud.

"We could make ornaments from the pieces of wood and material," Rebecca added.

"And Austin, I feel like the Whites are like family. Could we do something special for them?"

"What would you like to do?"

"Could we have them come over for dinner?"

"Would you be up to doing all that cooking? You're getting more pregnant every day, and I don't want you to overdo it."

"I'll plan the menu early and start making things in advance," she reassured him.

"The children could put on their little play for the Whites!" Austin exclaimed.

"Yes, that would be a good idea," Rebecca said, excitement showing in her voice.

Austin squeezed her hand, "This will be a Christmas to remember."

"What will we give the children from us? I could make mittens. I know how."

"If you want to do that, you can."

Rebecca smiled and stood up.

"Where are you going?"

"I can't wait a second longer. I want to get started right away!" She said, beaming.

The very next day, Rebecca and Austin began to help the children make their gifts.

"Shhh, Carrie, it's a secret!" Kristie said tiptoeing to the bedroom door. "We don't want Kelly Anne to know about her surprise."

Rebecca smiled at the girls. She was truly enjoying the preparation for their Christmas plans. "Here, Carrie, you can sew this dress. Just sew up the side like this." Rebecca handed the calico material to Carrie and showed her where to sew.

Then Rebecca handed Kristie material that they had cut out in the form of petticoats, and Kristie began following Rebecca's instructions.

In the barn, Austin was helping Kelly Anne to nail together pieces of wood to make a special bed for the twins' dolls. Earlier, Rebecca had helped her sew a piece of material to resemble a quilt.

Each night, Rebecca and Austin would share little bits of stories from their days of helping the children make their gifts.

"Then Kristie tiptoed over to the door and told Carrie to be quiet!" Rebecca told Austin excitedly. "They were so cute. They are so excited about making gifts for each other!"

"They're not the only ones!" Austin said with a twinkle in his eye as he grabbed his wife and spun her around.

Rebecca laughed, "I guess I'm excited, too. I never knew that being in a family could be so much fun."

"Wait until Christmas morning if you want to see excitement. When I was a child, we could hardly sleep. We kept sneaking out to see if our Mama and Papa were awake yet!"

"Oh, Austin, I can hardly wait!"

Rebecca danced around the room. Austin laughed and joined her.

"Well, Mrs. Finnigan, you are a fine dancer!" Austin exclaimed.

"Well, Mr. Finnigan, I have a fine dance partner!"

~*~

Several days later, Rebecca was pleasantly surprised at the sound of a wagon coming toward their home. There had been a break in the weather, and it had been several weeks since they had been able to attend church. Her heart quickened in hope of seeing her dear friend, Mrs. White. Her hope was fulfilled as she saw Austin helping the stout older woman from the wagon. Rebecca ran to the door and swung it open. Oh, she had so much to tell her dear friend.

Mrs. White looked at her and immediately said, "Something's different about you, Rebecca!"

"Oh, I can't hide anything from you," Rebecca said helping the woman off with her coat.

Mrs. White leaned over, picked up baby Ryan from the floor, and looked at Rebecca expectantly, "Well, out with it! You know I'm not very patient when it comes to hearing good news!"

"Oh, it's wonderful. Far greater than I ever believed or hoped. I asked Jesus to be my Savior!"

Mrs. White cried with glee, "Oh, Praise God! He has answered my prayers!" She looked intently at Rebecca saying, "Tell me everything!"

"Well, I told Austin how I was feeling, those same feelings that I had that day you wanted to talk to me. I just couldn't express my pain to you then. It hurt too much. But Austin and I have been reading the Bible together after the children go to bed each night. The Scriptures really came alive to me, but I still felt so empty. I finally told Austin how I felt, and he told me how to fill that emptiness."

Rebecca seemed to glow with excitement at the news she shared. Ryan reached out his arms and she took him and hugged him. "Oh, Mrs. White, I am so happy!"

Mrs. White reached out her hand and patted the young girl on the arm, "You deserve to be honey. You have had a rough life."

"Oh, I wish Mama could know the peace that I feel."

"Just your Mama? What about your father?"

"My father? He's the reason that I have suffered all this time. He does not deserve to have God."

"He, too, must have a reason for his anger. He, too, needs Jesus to heal him."

"But God is mine. I don't want to share Him with my cruel father. He took away all that my mother ever had. He gave me nothing."

The ever-present tears formed again in Rebecca's eyes. This time they were tears of anger not of hurt. Why would Mrs. White suggest such a thing? She was sorry that she had even talked to her about her new found faith. The peace and joy that she had experienced the last few days diminished, and she held the baby close to her and wept freely. Would her suffering never end?

"No one deserves to die in their sin," Mrs. White said softly. "God was willing to forgive, even those that crucified His Only Son."

Rebecca did not answer but released the baby as he began to squirm. She allowed him to get down from her lap, and she collapsed onto the table.

"Satan has blinded your father to the true way to behave. He has allowed liquor to control him. Did you ever wonder why he did some of the things that he did?" Mrs. White continued gently.

Rebecca's voice faltered in response. "I...I...asked Mama once about him. She said that he was sad for what his Papa had done to him. I could not understand why he didn't treat me better if his father treated him poorly. He should have remembered how hurt he had been as a child and treated me differently."

"Sometimes sin repeats itself, from father to son, mother to daughter. You responded in much the same way as your mother did, in fear and complete and absolute submission. If Austin was not a good man, would you have lived the same life your mother did?"

Rebecca realized that she would never have escaped Austin if he had abused her as her father did. She had made plans to do so, but in the end she knew she would have been too fearful to follow through. She looked up at Mrs. White with revelation on her face, "What do I need to do? How do I get rid of the anger I feel for my father?"

"You have to forgive him, dear." Mrs. White replied gently.

Rebecca gasped. How could she do that? "I cannot do that!" she exclaimed and stood up abruptly from her chair. The chair flew back with such a force it landed backwards with a thud that caused the baby to cry in fear. Rebecca knelt down and picked the child up, cuddling and whispering words of peace to him. She refused to look at Mrs. White who sat patiently as Rebecca consoled the child.

"By your own strength, you cannot; only God can do it through you. If you do not allow Him to do it, you will be a prisoner of your unforgiveness. You need to ask God to forgive you for hating your father. It's the only way to release your anger toward him and be freed from the pain of your past"

At that, Austin and the girls came in the door. Austin looked at his wife and the chair on the floor. He gave a questioning look to Mrs. White. Rebecca carried Ryan to the other room and changed his diaper, trying to get control of her emotions. Austin followed her to the room and stood above her. Rebecca ignored her husband and placed the baby on the bed. Austin placed his hands on her shoulders. She straightened but did not turn toward him.

"What's wrong, darling?" he whispered.

"Something I need to work out myself," she answered sadly. She turned toward him and buried her head in his shirt. "Oh," she wept. "Will the crying ever cease?"

"NOT UNTIL I HAVE HEALED YOU FROM ALL YOUR PAIN."

She gasped. "Did you say something, Austin?" she asked knowing that he had not. Was that God speaking to her? Somehow she knew it would take a miracle, a personal Word from Him to bring her to the point of forgiving her father. Maybe Mrs. White was right. Maybe it was time to let her anger go.

Somberly she turned toward the bed and got down on her knees. Austin picked up the baby and turned to go. Rebecca reached out her hand and grabbed his. He nodded and carried the baby out to Mrs. White and returned to his wife, and kneeling down beside her. She wept as she prayed, "Lord, I ask you to forgive me for my feelings toward my father." The words spoken gave such a release to Rebecca that she looked at Austin with surprise. "Lord, I..." she paused to take a deep breath, then said simply, "I forgive him."

Rebecca knew that this moment was not the last step to wholeness she desired, but one of many along the path that led there. She smiled at Austin beside her and thanked God again for the man he had given her to be her husband.

As Austin hugged his wife, he prayed for her parents, that they would come to know Christ as their daughter had. Rebecca agreed with him and the couple said amen in unison.

They returned to the kitchen, and Mrs. White did not need to ask what had happened in private. She saw the freedom written on Rebecca's face. She silently thanked the Lord for His continued guidance and provision.

~*~

When Austin and Rebecca felt it was time to tell the children about their little Christmas play and their guests, the children were excited. Austin retold the story, and from the start both twins wanted to be Mary.

Kelly Anne made the final decision clear, "I think Mama and Papa should be Joseph and Mary."

"Why Kelly Anne?" asked Austin curious about her choice.

"Because Papa is a man just like Joseph, and Mama has a baby in her tummy just like Mary did!"

The twins agreed and Austin and Rebecca conceded to their wishes.

Ryan, of course, would play the baby Jesus. Kristie would play the angel and Kelly Anne would be a shepherd. Carrie would play the inn keeper.

The family spent hours going over the story and deciding what each person would say. They made outfits to wear and props to use. They practiced and practiced, so much that Rebecca lay awake at night with the words and actions stirring in her head.

The Whites had graciously accepted the invitation and began praying for good weather. Mrs. White convinced Rebecca that she needed help with the food, especially in her pregnant condition. Rebecca conceded, and the two women planned the menu together.

Christmas day dawned with only last minute preparations left to complete. The gifts were all made and hidden away. The air was clear; it appeared that their prayers had been answered for good weather. The girls woke up at the first light and had run into Austin and Rebecca's bedroom.

"Mama, Papa," they yelled, "Merry Christmas. It's Jesus's birthday! Wake up!"

Austin pretended not to wake up, and Rebecca motioned for the girls to come in and rouse him. The girls started bouncing on top of their father. In one big move and lots of squeals, Austin grabbed all three girls at once and began tickling them. Rebecca laughed right along with the girls and then went to get the baby who had been awakened by all the fun.

Ryan was a docile baby and even when first awakened he always seemed to be in a cheerful mood. Austin reached out his arms for his son and Rebecca handed him over. Ryan grinned and giggled at his father.

"Rebecca, get the Bible, and we'll read the story of Jesus's birthday to start the day."

Rebecca got the Bible and climbed into the overcrowded bed. After a time of giggles and wiggles, the whole family was settled.

Austin opened the Bible and read the story that had become so familiar to the girls since they started practicing the play. In several places one of the girls would complete Austin's sentence. He smiled at their knowledge of the story.

When he finished, Austin closed the Bible, and said, "God gave us the gift of His Son, and we give gifts to each other to celebrate.

Let's all get our gifts and meet out in front of the tree!"

The girls giggled and scampered to their hiding places to retrieve the result of weeks of secrets and labors of love.

Each member of the family was pleasantly surprised at the gifts he/she had received. Rebecca noticed that the children seemed more excited about giving their gifts they had worked hard on much more than they were when they received one. It warmed her heart to see their joy.

Rebecca had made several things for Austin, warm slippers, gloves, a scarf, and a bookmark made of material left over from her wedding dress. She had embroidered, "Austin and Rebecca Finnigan" on it. Austin smiled and looked at her after he opened it. She hoped that he got the message that she was trying to portray. She wanted him to know that she wanted them to be together, man and wife, forever. His eyes twinkled, and he leaned over to kiss her cheek saying, "Is this for our Bible?"

"Yes, it's to mark where you and I are reading together."

"Now for your gift," Austin said with a twinkle in his eye. Rebecca waited impatiently as Austin went to the barn and came back with something covered up by a quilt.

"I think we're going to need two of these soon," he said as he placed the bulky gift on the floor.

Rebecca stood still and looked at him.

"Go ahead, look under the quilt."

Rebecca gingerly pulled up the quilt and squealed in surprise.

"I made it just for you!" Austin exclaimed.

Rebecca looked at the rocker. It looked so comfortable. Carved on the wood panel at the top of the back was Rebecca's name.

"I should have carved His on the old one and Hers on the new one. I have a feeling we both will be using them at the same time."

Rebecca just stood staring at the rocker. No one had ever given her a gift like this. Some years, her mother had smuggled her a piece of fruit or made her a doll from scraps, but nothing like this had ever been given to her before.

"Austin, it's beautiful," Rebecca croaked, barely able to speak."

"Come on, try it out," Austin said standing behind the rocker. Rebecca sat down, and Austin picked up the baby and handed him to her.

"You look like you belong there!" Austin said.

All three of the girls wanted to sit on Mama's lap and try the new rocking chair. Rebecca rocked each one of them and gave them a hug and a kiss.

After holding each child, Rebecca and her family changed into their Sunday best and waited impatiently for the Whites to arrive. Austin helped Rebecca with last minute preparations as much as he could. He did not allow her to lift anything. He was thankful that he had found two wild turkeys down at the creek just the week before and relished the smell of them roasting in the oven.

The sky was clear, and Rebecca rejoiced that the weather would not spoil their day. Around noon the children heard the wagon approaching and raced to the door. Rebecca did not allow them to open it until the moment their visitors were standing before it. It would take a while to warm the house after having the door open.

Rebecca hugged Mrs. White and each of the children. Each one of them held some delectable food item. Rebecca placed the dishes with her own food. Austin went out to help Mr. White get his horse team settled in the barn.

Rebecca and Mrs. White quickly set out to put the finishing touches on the food. The grownups sat down around the table and the children sat down on the floor. Austin said grace, thanking God for a good harvest that made the meal possible, and then he invited everyone to dig in.

There was so much food that the children squealed with glee. There were, of course, only four drumsticks, so Austin gave them to the four oldest children. There were mashed turnips, roasted yams, vegetables from the summer's garden, warm bread, and much more. Everyone ate until they didn't think they could eat any more only to see Rebecca carrying the pies to the table. All of a sudden, everyone had room for dessert.

After the meal was finished and the food put away, the Finnigan children went to change into their homemade costumes.

Rebecca looked with pride as they re-enacted the birth of Christ together. The story was relived with little prompting from Austin or Rebecca. Ryan decided to cry at just the wrong time and everyone laughed when the shepherd said sternly, "Baby Jesus, be still!"

At the end of the presentation the White family applauded and said they had never seen such a wonderful performance before. The children did not want to change out of their costumes, so they all continued to wear them except for Ryan who didn't find the swaddling clothes to his liking.

After the play, the family began to play games: Bean's Porridge Hot, Pussy in the Corner, Hide-and-Seek and a few games that the girls had made up. The Whites had given the Finnigan's a checker game for a Christmas gift and a tournament began immediately. Rebecca had never played before but learned quickly.

Rebecca hated for the day to end, but after a while the Whites bid the family good-bye. They did not know when they would see each other again. With prayers for a good winter and a promise to see each other as soon as they could, the families parted.

Later that night, although fatigue overwhelmed her body, Rebecca lay awake beside Austin, reliving each part of the special day. Austin sensed that she was not asleep.

He leaned up on his elbow and whispered in her ear, "Well, Mrs. Finnigan, did we make a good memory of Christmas pasts?"

"Oh, yes, Austin, we did. We surely did!"

He held her in his arms and felt her soften at his touch. She fell asleep with a smile on her face.

~*~

Rebecca stood at the window as she watched the light from Austin's lantern move toward the barn. It had been snowing steadily all day, and Austin had gone to the barn to check the livestock. There were several inches of snow on the ground already, and Austin warned her that by morning she would see much more.

She turned from the window and placed her hands on her aching back. She lowered herself into a chair and sighed. She was so uncomfortable, and no matter what she did she could not find relief.

She heard Ryan cry from the other room and reluctantly rose from the chair and made her way to his bed. She smiled down at the little boy. Lately, he had been crawling all over the place and she found herself scrambling to grab things left behind by the girls. She leaned over him and picked him up, softly singing to him a hymn she had learned in church. She loved this little boy as if he were her own. Could she possibly love the baby in her womb anymore?

She changed his diaper and began feeding him as she sat down in the rocker. He looked at her and reached up and grabbed a handful of her thick curly hair. She met his gaze and smiled at him. She loved it when he held her hair as she fed him. She continued to rock and sing to him as his eyes grew heavy and finally closed. He continued to suck until the bottle was empty.

Rebecca did not want to end this moment and continued to rock him. Austin entered the house and saw the mother and child, and his heart burst with love for the woman who had entered his life and stole his heart. He thanked God for sending her to him and for her love for their children. He took off his snowy boots and crept over beside the pair.

He knelt down and reached out to touch the hair that his son loved as much as he did. He wished that she would keep it down all the time instead of that bun she pulled it back into during the day. He smiled. No matter how hard she tried to tame it, loose tendrils would escape the bun and dangle down her forehead and in front of her ears. She was forever trying to tuck it back in, but it was a losing battle with Austin and Ryan always trying to release it from its bondage.

The couple stared at the sleeping baby for a few minutes, and then Austin took him from her and carried him to his bed. He returned to her and knelt before her, placing his hands on her swollen stomach.

"We'll soon be taking care of another one," he said softly.

She smiled at him. It always surprised her when he acted like this child was theirs together. He had accepted the new baby as his own, just like he had accepted her as his own. The baby kicked as if in response to his father's hands so near. Austin laughed and talked to the baby.

"Hey little one. We're waiting for you out here. We can't wait to meet you. It's a great place out here with a mama and papa who love you and lots of sisters and a brother, too!"

Rebecca giggled at the thought of the little baby being overwhelmed by his new family. "One look at all of us and he's going to want to go back to that safe place he had!" she said, smiling.

Austin pretended to look hurt, "Why, Mrs. Finnigan, are you implying that our little family is overwhelming?"

"Why no, Mr. Finnigan, I am not implying anything. It is a fact!"

"If this child is anything like his mother, he'll adjust quickly and get along just fine," Austin said as he stood and pulled his wife out of the rocker and to him.

"I'm excited," Austin said with a grin. "With the blizzard, I have no reason to leave the house. I won't need to make up excuses to come back in just to get a glimpse of you!"

Rebecca hadn't realized that he had been doing that. His words sent a warm glow through her at the thought of him wanting to see her so often.

"Come, Mrs. Finnigan, you need your rest," he said leading her into the bedroom.

But Rebecca did not get much rest that night. She could not get comfortable and felt pains in her abdomen. She tried to keep them from Austin who was sleeping soundly beside her. She did not want to disturb his sleep, but eventually the pain became so severe that she cried out. Austin awoke with a start to find her drenched in sweat beside him.

"Rebecca, are you in labor?"

"I...I...don't know. I think so. What does it feel like?"

Austin laughed nervously, "I don't know, but it looks like what you're going through right now."

His worried eyes met hers, and he tried to conceal his concern. It was the time he had feared since the day he asked her to be his wife. Could he make it through another birthing? What if she had trouble? He could not bear to lose her or the baby. He strode to the window and found that there was too much snow for him to go for Mrs. White. They had known that the possibility was great that Austin would be alone to deliver the baby, so Mrs. White had given him instructions. But fear gripped his heart at the thought of it being his responsibility to deliver this new life and keep his wife safe.

He knelt down beside Rebecca, and she reached out her hand to try to wipe the worried look from his eyes. He took her hand and kissed her palm.

"Don't be afraid, Austin. Pray. I know that God will hear us and protect me and the baby."

"I've been praying for months for this day."

Austin tried to make Rebecca comfortable as they waited out the hours of labor pains. He rubbed her back and propped her up with pillows. When he wasn't making her more comfortable, he was on his knees praying or reading the Bible to her.

The morning light shone brightly through the window as it reflected off the falling snow. Austin wiped the sweat from Rebecca's face and examined her.

"I see the baby's head," he exclaimed, "Come on darling, push."

Rebecca was exhausted and wanted to give up, but Austin's encouraging words each time made her obey him.

Finally he said, "One, more, Rebecca. Come on you can do it!"

Rebecca pulled herself up and gave the hardest push she was capable of and then fell back on the pillows.

"He's out, Rebecca. It's a boy!" Austin held the baby up to show his wife, and then quickly followed Mrs. White's instructions to help the baby breathe its first breath.

Rebecca pulled herself up to watch Austin and held her own breath waiting. The baby gave out a lusty cry, and Rebecca wept tears of gratefulness as she lay back down on the bed, utterly exhausted.

Austin wrapped the baby in a clean cloth and placed him on Rebecca's chest. She cried softly as she looked at the life that had been growing inside of her. An overwhelming love flooded through her, and she knew that God had answered her prayers. She could easily love this baby!

As Austin tended to Rebecca's needs, she held the baby close to herself and dozed in exhaustion. Austin heard whispers from the other room. He peeked out to see the girls awake and looking at him.

"We heard a baby crying, Papa. We knew it wasn't Ryan. Is it our new baby?"

"Yes, children, you have another little brother."

Remembering what happened to their first mama when Ryan was born the children anxiously asked, "Mama, Mama, are you okay?"

"Your mama is fine. Do you want to see her?"

The girls scrambled to the door. Austin smiled at their anxiousness and told them to be quiet.

Rebecca opened her eyes and smiled at the children.

"Mama," Carrie cried, "You didn't go to heaven. We were afraid you were going to go to heaven like our first mama."

"No, my darlings, I wouldn't leave you. God knows how much I need you!"

"Silly, Mama, we need you," bossy Kristie said.

"I think I need you more, honey."

Rebecca turned the baby for the girls to see and they gasped, "He's so little."

"Yes he is, but not for long, if he wants to keep up with his brother and sisters," Austin remarked. "Now, come girls and let Mama and the baby get some sleep."

Rebecca closed her eyes and was instantly asleep. She was so tired. She did not stir again until she heard Ryan's cries from the other room. Austin carried him into the room. "I knew that you wouldn't be able to stay in bed if I didn't bring him into you. He seemed really upset when he didn't see you this morning. I couldn't quiet him down or even get him to eat! Looks like you now have two babies who need you!"

She smiled as Austin sat down on the bed beside her. She reached out for Ryan, and Austin took the new baby from her. He looked him over and felt the same pride fill his being that had done so three times before in his life.

"What shall we name him, Mrs. Finnigan?" he said looking over at Rebecca.

"I would like to name him, Austin James Finnigan, junior."

Austin grinned from ear to ear at her suggestion. He knew that she wanted this baby to be his own as much as he did. "Hello, little Austin. Welcome home," he said peering down at the boy.

Austin went over to one of his drawers and pulled out a wrapped package. "This is for you, Rebecca. It's your keepsake to pass on, and it's a reminder of how much I love you!"

Rebecca looked at him with surprise and took the package. Austin took Ryan from her arms and placed him in the waiting cradle. She opened the gift slowly to reveal a delicate gold necklace etched with roses.

"Oh, Austin it's beautiful. I don't know what to say."

"Here, I'll help you put it on."

Rebecca leaned forward for him to put it around her neck and Austin leaned down and clumsily fumbled with the clasp. He eventually got it open, placed it around her neck, and closed the clasp again. Then he leaned over and kissed her on the neck. It caused tingles to go through Rebecca. He sat down beside her and kissed her face and her lips. "I'm so proud of you, Rebecca. I love you."

"I love you, too, Austin," Rebecca said returning his kisses.

But then she began to cry.

"What's wrong, honey?"

"I never thought that when I ran away from Ireland I would end up being so happy! When I met your sister on the ship, I just resigned myself to a life of working for others. I hoped, even dreamed, of happiness, but I never truly thought it was within my grasp. I really thought God was punishing me for being a bad girl."

"Oh, sweetheart, there isn't one bad thing in you. You are a wonderful wife and a loving mother."

"I know now that God was not punishing me. It took a long time to realize that, but I'm so happy now, I know He only wants the best for me."

"I'm glad that His best included me! What would I do without you?"

"Well, you would wash dishes, wash clothes, change diapers, cook..."

Austin laughed, "Yes, I'd be doing all those things, but don't think for a second that's all that I need you for." He took her hands and kissed them, "I need your smile, I need your laughter, I need your tender touch. I need to wake up in the middle of the night and hear you breathing softly and feel you lying beside me. I need your excitement over a verse in the Bible that you never heard before. Why Rebecca, I need you, not for what you do for me, but who you are to me! You make me happy!"

"Oh, Austin," Rebecca wept as he drew her into his arms. She never wanted to be out of his arms, and they held each other in silence for a long time.

Rebecca was up and around in a few days, but grateful that Austin was stranded in the house to help her. She had her hands full with two babies and was overwhelmed with the time it took to keep the two of them dry and fed. Still, she would not trade the feeling of joy and pride she felt over her new son. Not a day went by that she did not thank God for him and for providing him with a good father in Austin.

Chapter 17

*S*igns of spring were popping up all over. Austin, Jr., was two months old and the family was experiencing cabin fever. The girls followed their father to the barn to help with chores. Although their "help" was more of a hindrance, he did not mind. He was full of joy at his growing family. He smiled as Carrie lifted the scoop to give the cow some feed. Kristie ran to gather the eggs and feed the chickens. Kelly Anne stood by watching to learn how Austin milked the cow. He smiled at her, and she giggled.

Austin walked back toward the house and surveyed its size. He knew that he must build an addition. His little family was bursting at the seams. There was only one room for the children, and once Baby Austin was moved out of their bedroom there would be no room left. Then there was the possibility of future children? Austin frowned. Would they have any children together? Would this platonic relationship continue as it had been? He prayed that someday he could be a true husband to Rebecca as it was meant to be. He had promised God that he would wait for her as long as it took, but he ached so for her. He could hardly bare to sleep beside her each night. He loved her so! "Oh, Lord," he prayed silently, "give me the strength to keep on doing what you have commanded me to do." He had waited for her to have the baby and these last few months had been very hard on them both with several night feedings. Rebecca collapsed into bed at night. He knew it was not yet time to bring his love to completion with her. He shook off the desire to sulk in impatience and walked back to the house.

~*~

The next day Austin began cutting trees by the creek and hauling them to the house. On the days that followed, he worked on the house. Mr. White and his son came over and helped. Soon the room was built. The final step was to cut a hole in the original wall to make a door.

Rebecca was excited about the new room. It had been decided that it would be hers and Austin's. She could decorate it as she desired. She had started a quilt before the baby came and hoped to have it finished before they moved into the new room. Together they had decided that she could use some of her money to buy new furnishings, so they had poured over catalogues to find just the right pieces. She had made curtains to match the quilt and was anxious to hang them.

With the room completed and the bed moved in, Rebecca felt as if their life together had truly become theirs alone. She did not have to share her bedroom with the memories of Victoria. She finally felt like this was her family and her home.

That first night, Austin crawled into the new bed beside Rebecca. It was getting harder for him to sleep beside her without showing her how much he loved her. Although he had felt she might have been ready months ago, her pregnancy had stopped him from approaching her. He slept restlessly with her slim body so close to his. He knew that the children exhausted her, but the reasons for withholding his passions did not stop the desire from rising within him.

Rebecca had always slept with her back to him, and although she had long stopped tensing in fear at his touch, she was reluctant to give him any sign that she was ready for more than the occasional kisses and hugs he gave her. Part of her longed to give herself fully to him but fear held her back.

Austin's restlessness kept Rebecca awake most of the night, and before the light even peeked through the window, she rose and left the room. She knelt down before the fire and stoked it up to take the chill from the small house. She did not rise immediately, but knelt there praying for her children and her husband. She knew that it was time to let go of her fear once and for all and to give herself freely to him. She loved and trusted him, and she wanted to show it in this intimate way, but she did not know how to tell him. She prayed for the right words and for courage to express her desires for him.

She did not hear Austin enter the room and jumped at his touch on her shoulder. He turned to leave, feeling an overwhelming rejection course through him. Would she ever accept him in all ways as her husband? As he turned away, she reached out her hand and grabbed his. He turned and looked at her. She pulled on his hand, and he knelt down in front of her facing her. She reached up and touched his face. She looked into his loving eyes. "I love you, Austin. I want to be your wife in every way!" she said boldly, her words sounding more confident than she truly was. She smiled softly.

Pleasantly surprised, Austin said, "I love you, Rebecca, my darling. Are you sure you're ready?" As he asked the question, he was fearful of the answer.

"Oh, darling, we've waited oh so long. Can you forgive me? I know that my past experience frightens me. But you are different. I love you and I know this is a way to express my love to you. I am not afraid."

"It is a reflection of my love for you as well," he said tenderly. "I would not do anything to hurt you. Anything that happened in the past was not out of love. Do you understand that? Can you trust me to show you my love in this way?"

"Yes, Austin, I can," she replied.

Rebecca stood, knowing that she truly had nothing to fear. This wonderful man loved her so. God had kept her "in His hands" and blessed her with Austin. She thanked God for His care and provision. She embraced her husband as he led her to their bedroom to make a new memory: love's memory.

ABOUT THE AUTHOR

Living in the same small western Pennsylvania town where she was raised, Diana has been an elementary school teacher for over 30 years. She loves studying the Bible with her class and helping students master tough concepts. They are encouraged to never give up or let discouragement rob them. This is the theme of Diana's book, *Love's Memory.*

Diana is involved in her local church, Kiski Valley Assembly of God, where she teaches adult growth groups using Precept Ministry Bible studies by founder Kay Arthur. She loves reaching out to underprivileged children through the ministry of Samaritan's Purse where she has encourages others to pack Operation Christmas Child shoe boxes.

Diana has been married for 35 years to Jamie, a man whose godly life continues to bless and enrich her. His encouragement gave her courage to pursue her dream of being an author. Diana often says that Jamie is the best gift God ever gave her. Diana and Jamie raised one son, Jim, and have two grandchildren, Brittany and BJ.

You may contact Diana at www.lambbooks.com

Mom's Buns and Cinnamon Rolls
by Gail Pugh

One of my best childhood memories was of Mom making these buns. I would watch her knead the dough with her strong arms and hands. The smell of them baking would bring us to the kitchen. They were delicious especially warm from the oven smothered in butter!

Stir and then leave sit 10 minutes:
1/2 cup warm water
Sprinkle 2 dry yeast packets over water
Stir in 2 TB Sugar

Add:
4 cups warm water
1 cup oil
1 TB salt
1 1/2 cups sugar

Stir it up.

Add 8 cups flour and mix.
Add 4 more cups of flour and mix.
Knead in 2 more cups of flour.
Sprinkle 1 cup of flour on clean counter and knead the dough there.

Continue adding flour until dough is not sticky.

Place in bowl and let raise. Punch it down. Let it raise again.

Divide dough up into 4-5 pieces. Take one piece at a time and pinch off a small piece (to make bun-remember it will raise), flatten with your hand and place on *greased* cookie sheet. After placing buns on cookie sheet press down again. Cover with a clean cloth (tea towels, table cloth, etc).

Raise for 5-6 hours. Bake at 375 degrees for rebece2-15 minutes until desired brown color. Take rolls out and brush on top of rolls with softened butter.

For cinnamon rolls; instead of bun shapes roll the handful of dough into a long roll. Spread generously with softened butter, add sugar and brown sugar and press into butter slightly. Sprinkle with cinnamon.

Raise for 5-6 hours. Bake at 375 degrees until desired brown color.

When cool add Powdered Sugar Icing:

1 cup powdered sugar
1/2 teaspoon vanilla
1-2 tablespoons milk- add slowly until the mixture is the consistency that is easily spreadable.

   Yummy! Enjoy!
   -Diana Barclay

www.ingramcontent.com/pod-product-compliance
Lightning Source LLC
Chambersburg PA
CBHW060421180626
46817CB00007B/2613